EVERYMAN,

I WILL GO WITH THEE,

AND BE THY GUIDE,

IN THY MOST NEED

TO GO BY THY SIDE

✳

# JOHN UPDIKE

# OLINGER
# STORIES

## A SELECTION

EVERYMAN'S POCKET CLASSICS

Alfred A. Knopf  New York  London  Toronto

THIS IS A BORZOI BOOK
PUBLISHED BY ALFRED A. KNOPF

www.randomhouse.com/knopf/classics
www.everymanslibrary.co.uk

ISBN: 978-0-375-71250-0 (US)
978-1-84159-618-1 (UK)

A CIP catalogue reference for this book is available from the
British Library

Typography by Peter B. Willberg
Typeset in the UK by AccComputing, Wincanton, Somerset
Printed and bound in Germany by GGP Media GmbH, Pössneck

# OLINGER STORIES

# CONTENTS

# PUBLISHER'S NOTE

OLINGER STORIES is John Updike's own selection from his first eight years of *New Yorker* fiction, 1954–62. It was originally published, as a rack-sized paperback original, by Vintage Books, New York, in the fall of 1964. This Everyman's edition, issued to commemorate the book's fiftieth anniversary, marks its first appearance in hardcover.

When Updike assembled his omnibus *The Early Stories* in 2002, he arranged the material in eight sections, with the Olinger stories making up the first of them. As he wrote in the foreword to that omnibus, the prospect of collecting his early stories presented to him no satisfaction stronger than that of "seeing *Olinger Stories* back together." (The book had long been out of print, he commented in an aside, "though a few professors who used to assign it have complained.") These eleven stories were not conceived as a series, he continued, but do seem to "constitute a green and slender whole," for all of them spring from the same autobiographical soil – "the only child, the small town, the grandparental home, the move in adolescence to a farm." The book was dear to its author; he considered it his signature collection, the volume of short stories that communicated his freshest impressions of life as it came to him in hardscrabble Berks County, Pennsylvania, in the 1930s and '40s. "This is the way it was, *is*."

The texts of the stories reprinted here are those that Updike published in *The Early Stories*, which he deemed

9

definitive. The foreword is that of the original Vintage edition of *Olinger Stories*, altered only to incorporate a few small changes made by the author after its initial publication. It is perhaps worth noting, as a gloss on that foreword, that the last story here, "In Football Season," was first collected in *Olinger Stories* and later used as the opening story of Updike's 1966 collection *The Music School*.

*October 2013*

# FOREWORD TO THE
# VINTAGE EDITION

THREE OF THESE STORIES are from my collection *The Same Door*; seven are from *Pigeon Feathers and Other Stories*; and one, the last, has not previously been included in any book. All were first printed in *The New Yorker*. They have been arranged here in the order of the hero's age; in the beginning he is ten, in the middle stories he is an adolescent, in the end he has reached manhood. He wears different names and his circumstances vary, but he is at bottom the same boy, a local boy – this selection could be called *A Local Boy*. The locality is that of Olinger, Pennsylvania, a small town bounded on the urban side by Alton and on the rural side by Firetown. The name Olinger (pronounced with a long *O*, a hard *g*, and the emphasis on the first syllable) was coined, to cap a rebuke, in a story called "The Alligators":

"You're not in Baltimore now, Joan," Miss Fritz said. "You are in Olinger, Pennsylvania."

The name is audibly a shadow of "Shillington," the real name of my home town, yet the two towns, however similar, are not at all the same. Shillington is a place on the map and belongs to the world; Olinger is a state of mind, of my mind, and belongs entirely to me.

When the idea was first proposed – in a kind and thoughtful letter from Mr. John F. Horty, Jr., of Philadelphia – that my "Olinger stories" be printed in one paperback volume, my publishers were agreeable but I hesitated. My other collections were still amply for sale, and an anthology derived from them, especially by me, seemed fussy. In the matter of arranging short stories, I think the order in which they were written is the most natural and normally useful. A more pointed arrangement, seeking to reveal some inner consistency, could not help but point up inconsistencies of detail. Further, not all of the stories whose spiritual center is Olinger take place there. And further still, the book would be slim.

From the fact of the slim book in your hand you may deduce that my doubts were not conclusive. They succumbed to the hope that a concentration of certain images might generate new light, or at least focus more sharply the light already there. I hope that this book is justified. I bind these stories together as one ties up a packet of love letters that have been returned. Olinger has receded from me. Composition, in crystallizing memory, displaces it, and the town and the time it localizes have been consumed by the stories bound here. Not an autobiography, they have made one impossible. In the last of them, Olinger has become "like a town in a fable"; and in my novel *The Centaur*, by turning Olinger explicitly into Olympus, I intended to say the final word, and farewell. Perhaps I exaggerate; it is an inherited fault. But the most recent piece here, "In Football Season," was written over two years ago, and I offer this book in the faith that it is a closed book.

The oldest story is "Friends from Philadelphia." It was the first story I ever sold, and I wrote it in Vermont, on my father-in-law's typewriter, in the June of my graduation from college. I had given myself five years to become a "writer," and my becoming one immediately has left me with an uneasy, apologetic sense of having blundered through the wrong door. Nevertheless, it is a story I am grateful to, and it has remained, for all my zealous subsequent activity, my mother's favorite. In it, Olinger, unnamed, is simply the world; its author is so young that everything outside Olinger – Harvard, marriage, Vermont – seemed relatively unreal, and in his innocence he gave the heroine a last name, Lutz, which people outside the Pennsylvania Dutch counties pronounce to rhyme with "guts" instead of, correctly, with "Toots." I have been told that the story seems to have no point. The point, to me, is plain, and is the point, more or less, of all these Olinger stories. *We are rewarded unexpectedly.* The muddled and inconsequent surface of things now and then parts and yields us a gift. In my boyhood I had the impression of being surrounded by an incoherent generosity, of – to quote a barefaced reminiscence I once wrote –

> a quiet but tireless goodness that things at rest, like a brick wall or a small stone, seem to affirm. A wordless reassurance these things are pressing to give. An hallucination? To transcribe middleness with all its grits, bumps, and anonymities, in its fullness of satisfaction and mystery: is it possible or, in view of the suffering that violently colors the periphery and that at all moments threatens to move into the center, worth doing? Possibly not; but the horse-chestnut trees, the telephone poles, the porches, the green hedges recede to a calm point that in my subjective geography is still the center of the world.

Olinger, if it is like Shillington, is a square mile of middle-class homes physically distinguished by a bend in the central avenue that compels some side streets to deviate from the grid pattern. Its population numbers less than 5,000, predominantly Protestant and of German descent. (D. W. Brogan, in his book *The American Character*, remarks that "The Germans who settled in early Pennsylvania have stayed put ever since, and their fertile, well-formed, stable countryside often evokes nostalgia in European breasts. But America was not made by ways of life that evoke European nostalgia . . .") Olinger is west of greater Philadelphia and south of the coal regions and contains a box factory and a small hosiery mill which in World War II made parachutes. Most of its citizens look economically toward Alton, a middle-sized city whose industries are steel, textiles, pretzels, and beer. The surrounding land is loamy, and Olinger is haunted – hexed, perhaps – by rural memories, accents, and superstitions. Cars travelling through see nothing here to make them stop; the town is neither young nor old, poor nor rich, backward nor forward. It is beyond the western edge of Megalopolis, and hangs between its shallow hills enchanted, nowhere, anywhere; there is no place like it. Its children, however dispersed by military service and education, almost all return. I have returned often, though seldom bodily, and am delighted to report that the flags there still carry forty-eight stars, the pledge of allegiance omits "under God," and the Lord's Prayer is daily recited in the schools.

I have let the inconsistencies stand in these stories. Each started from scratch. Grand Avenue here is the Alton Pike there. In "Pigeon Feathers" the grandfather is dead, in "Flight" the grandmother. In fact, both of my mother's parents lived until I was an adult. In fact, my family moved eleven miles away from the town when I was thirteen; in "Friends from Philadelphia" the distance is one mile, in "The Happiest I've Been" it has grown to four. This strange distance, this less than total remove from my milieu, is for all I know the crucial detachment of my life. In some stories, like "Flight" and "A Sense of Shelter," I have pretended the physical distance did not exist, but it is there, as the enchantment that makes Molly Bingaman and Mary Landis unattainable.

The hero is always returning, from hundreds of miles finally. Only the first two stories show a pure Olinger child. It surprised me, in making this arrangement, to realize that the boy who wrestles with H. G. Wells and murders pigeons is younger than the one who tells Thelma Lutz she shouldn't pluck her eyebrows. But we age unevenly, more slowly in society than in our own skulls. Among these eleven brothers, some are twins. John Nordholm and David Kern, having taken their turn as actors, reappear as narrators. And optically bothered Clyde Behn seems to me a late refraction of that child Ben who flees the carnival with "tinted globes confusing his eyelashes."

It does not do to dote. Fiction must recommend itself or remain unrecommended. But if of my stories I had to pick a few to represent me, they would be, I suppose, for reasons only partially personal, these.

J. U.
*Ipswich, Mass.*
*April 1964*

# YOU'LL NEVER
# KNOW, DEAR, HOW
# MUCH I LOVE YOU

CARNIVAL! In the vacant lot behind the old ice plant! Trucks have been unloading all afternoon; the WhirloGig has been unfolded like a giant umbrella, they assembled the baby Ferris wheel with an Erector Set. Twice the trucks got stuck in the mud. Straw has been strewn everywhere. They put up a stage and strung lights. Now, now, gather your pennies; supper is over and an hour of light is left in the long summer day. See, Sammy Hunnenhauser is running; Gloria Gring and her gang have been there all afternoon, they never go home, oh hurry, let me go; how awful it is to have parents that are poor, and slow, and sad!

Fifty cents. The most Ben could beg. A nickel for every year of his life. It feels like plenty. Over the roof of crazy Mrs. Moffert's house, the Ferris wheel tints the air with pink, and the rim of this pink mixes in his excitement with the great notched rim of the coin sweating in his hand. This house, then this house, and past the ice plant, and he will be there. Already the rest of the world is there, he is the last, hurrying, hurrying, the balloon is about to take off, the Ferris wheel is lifting; only he will be left behind, on empty darkening streets.

Then there, what to buy? There are not so many people here. Grown-ups carrying babies mosey glassily on the straw walks. All the booth people, not really gypsies, stare at him, and beckon weakly. It hurts him to ignore the man with the three old softballs, and the old cripple at the merry-go-round, and the fat lady with her plaster Marys, and the skeleton suspended behind a fountain of popcorn. He feels his walking past them as pain. He wishes there were more people here; he feels a fool. All of this machinery assembled to extract from him his pathetic fifty cents. He watches at a distance a thickset man in earnestly rolled-up shirtsleeves twirl a great tinselled wheel with a rubber tongue that patters slower and slower on a circle of nails until it stops between two, and the number there wins. Only a sailor and two boys in yellow silk high-school athletic jackets play. None win. The thick tattooed arm below the rolled-up shirtsleeve care-fully sweeps their nickels from a long board divided and numbered as if for hopscotch. The high-school boys, with sideburns and spotty whiskers on their bright-pink jaws, put down nickels again leadenly, and this time the man spinning the wheel shouts when it stops, seems more joyful than they, and reaches into his deep apron pocket and pours before them, without counting, a perfect little slipping stack of nickels. Their gums showing as if at a dirty joke, the two boys turn – the shimmer on their backs darts and shifts in cool $z$'s – and walk away, while the man is shouting, "Hey, uh winneh. Hey, uh winneh, evvybody wins." His board is bare, and as his mouth continues to form the loud words his eyes lock Ben into a stare of heartbreaking brown blankness that seems to elucidate with paralyzing clarity Ben's state: his dungarees, his fifty cents, his ten years, his position in space, and above the particulars the immense tinted pity, the waste, of being at one little place instead of everywhere, at any time. Then the man looks away, and twirls the wheel for his own amusement.

The fifty-cent piece feels huge to Ben's fingers, a wide oppressive rigidity that must be broken, shattered into twinkling fragments, to merge in the tinsel and splinters of strewn straw. He buys, at the first stand he strikes, a cone of cotton candy, and receives, with the furry pink pasty uncoiling thing, a quarter, a dime, and a nickel: three coins, tripling his wealth.

Now people multiply, crowd in from the houses of the town, which stand beyond the lot on all sides in black forbidding silhouettes like the teeth of a saw. The lights go on; the faces of the houses flee. There is nothing in the lot but light, and at its core, on the stage, three girls wearing white cowboy hats and white spangled skirts and white boots appear, and a man also in white and bearing a white guitar strung with gold. The legs around Ben crush him toward the stage; the smell of mud mingles with the bright sight there. One of the girls coughs into the microphone and twists its neck, so a sharp whine pierces from the loud-speakers and cuts a great crescent through the crowd, leaving silence as harvest. The girls sing, toe-tapping gingerly: "The other *night*, dear, as I lay *sleep*ing, I dreamt I *held* you in my *arms*." The spangles on their swishing skirts spring prickles like tears in Ben's eyes. The three voices sob, catch, twang, distend his heart like a rubber band at the highest pitch of their plaint. "– I was mis*tak*en, and I *hung* my *head*, a-and *cried*." And then the unbearable rising sugar of the chorus that makes his scalp so tight he fears his head will burst from sweet fullness.

The girls go on to sing other songs, less good, and then they give way to a thin old man in suspenders and huge pants he keeps snapping and looking down and whooping into. He tells horrible jokes that make the nice fat ladies standing around Ben – nice fat factory and dust-mop women that made him feel protected – shake with laughter. He fears their quaking, feels threatened from beneath, as if there is a treacherous stratum under this mud and straw. He wanders away, to let the words of "You Are My Sunshine" revolve in his head. "Please don't *take* my *sun*shine a*way*." Only the money in his pocket weighs him; get rid of it, and he will sail away like a dandelion seed.

He goes to the booth where the wheel is turning, and puts his nickel on the board in a square marked 7, and loses it.

He puts the dime there, and it too is taken away.

Squeezed, almost hidden, between the crusty trousered haunches of two adults, he puts down his quarter, as they do, on the inner edge, to be changed. The tattooed man comes along, picking up the quarters and pouring, with his wonderfully automatic fingers, the little slipping stacks of five nickels; Ben holds his breath, and to his horror feels his low face catch in the corner of the man's absent-minded eyes. The thick solemn body snags in its smooth progress, and Ben's five nickels are raggedly spaced. Between the second and third there is a gap. A blush cakes Ben's cheeks; his gray-knuckled fingers, as they push out a nickel, are trembling sideways at each other. But the man goes back, and spins the wheel, and Ben loses three nickels one after another. The twittering wheel is a moon-faced god; but Ben feels humanity clouding the space between him and it, which should be unobstructed. When the tattooed arm – a blue fish, an anchor, the queer word PEACE – comes to sweep in his nickels, he feels the stippled skin breathing thought, and lowers his head against the expected fall of words. Nothing is said, the man moves on, returns to the wheel; but Ben feels puzzled pressure radiating from him, and the pointed eyes of a man in a suit with chalk stripes who has come to stand at the far side of the stand intersect this expanding circle, and Ben, hurrying to pour his money down a narrowing crack, puts down his last two nickels, still on 7.

The rubber tongue leaps into pattering and as the wheel whirls the tattooed man leans backward to hear the one in chalk stripes talk; this one's tongue patters silently but a tiny motion of his smooth hand, simultaneous with a sideways stab of his eyes, is toward Ben.

The rubber tongue slows, flops, stops at 7 – no, 8. He lost, and can leave. The floor of his stomach lifts queerly. "Hey, kid." The man with terrible spoiled arms comes over. Ben feels that no matter how fast he would run those arms would stretch and snare him.

"Huh?"

"How old are you, kid?"

"Ten."

"Whatsamatta with ya, ya daddy rich?"

A titter moves stiffly among the immense adult heads all around. Ben understands the familiar role, that he has undergone a hundred times with teachers and older boys, of being a comic prop. He understands everything, and wants to explain that he knows his eyes are moist and his cheeks red but that it's because of joy, freedom, not because of losing. But this would be too many words; even the one-word answer "No" sticks to the roof of his mouth and comes loose with a faint tearing noise.

"Here." With his exciting expert touch, the tattooed man flicks Ben's two coins back across the painted number. Then he digs into his pocket. He comes up with the usual little stack of five, drops four, but holds the fifth delicately between the tips of two fingers and a thumb, hesitates so that Ben can reread PEACE in blue above his wrist, and then flips the fifth nickel up into his palm and thence down with a plunge into his dirty sagging apron pouch.

"Now move away from the board, kid, move away. Don't come back."

Ben fumbles the coins into his hands and pushes away, his eyes screwed to the sharp edge of painted wood, and he shoulders blindly backward through the legs. Yet all the time, in the midst of the heat and water welling up from springs all over his body, he is figuring, and calculates he's been gypped. Forty: he had the quarter and dime and nickel, and they gave him back only six nickels: thirty. The injustice. They pretend he's too little to lose and then keep a dime. The waste. The lost dime seems a tiny hole through which everything in existence is draining. As he moves away, his wet knees jarring, trying to hide forever from every sailor and fat woman and high-schooler who witnessed his disgrace, the six nickels make a knobbed weight bumping his thigh through his pocket. The spangles, the splinters of straw and strings of light, the sawtooth peaks of houses showing behind the heads of grown-ups moving above the scent of grassy mud are hung like the needles of a Christmas tree with the transparent, tinted globes confusing his eyelashes.

Thus the world, like a jaded coquette, spurns our attempts to give ourselves to her wholly.

# THE ALLIGATORS

JOAN EDISON came to their half of the fifth grade from Maryland in March. She had a thin face with something of a grown-up's tired expression and long black eyelashes like a doll's. Everybody hated her. That month Miss Fritz was reading to them during homeroom about a girl, Emmy, who was badly spoiled and always telling her parents lies about her twin sister, Annie; nobody could believe, it was too amazing, how exactly when they were despising Emmy most Joan should come into the school with her show-off clothes and her hair left hanging down the back of her fuzzy sweater instead of being cut or braided and her having the crust to actually argue with teachers. "Well, I'm sorry," she told Miss Fritz, not even rising from her seat, "but I *don't* see what the point is of homework. In Baltimore we never had any, and the *little* kids there knew what's in these books."

Charlie, who in a way enjoyed homework, was ready to join in the angry moan of the others. Little hurt lines had leaped up between Miss Fritz's eyebrows and he felt sorry for her, remembering how when, that September, John Eberly had half on purpose spilled purple Sho-Card paint on the newly sandpapered floor she had hidden her face in her arms on the desk and cried. She was afraid of the school board. "You're not in Baltimore now, Joan," Miss Fritz said. "You are in Olinger, Pennsylvania."

The children, Charlie among them, laughed, and Joan, blushing a soft brown color and raising her voice excitedly against the current of hatred, got in deeper by trying to explain, "Like there, instead of just *reading* about plants in a book, we'd one day all bring in a flower we'd *picked* and cut it open and look at it in a *microscope*." Because of her saying this, shadows, of broad leaves and wild slashed foreign flowers, darkened and complicated the idea they had of her.

Miss Fritz puckered her orange lips into fine wrinkles, then smiled. "In the upper levels you will be allowed to do that in this school. All things come in time, Joan, to patient little girls." When Joan started to argue *this*, Miss Fritz lifted one finger and said with that extra weight adults always have, held back in reserve, "No. No more, young lady, or you'll be in *serious* trouble with me." It gave the class courage to see that Miss Fritz didn't like her either.

After that, Joan couldn't open her mouth in class without there being a great groan. Outdoors on the macadam playground, at recess or fire drill or waiting in the morning for the buzzer, hardly anybody talked to her except to say "Stuck-up" or "Emmy" or, worst, "Whore, whore, from Balti-more." Boys were always yanking open the bow at the back of her fancy dresses and flipping little spitballs into the curls of her hanging hair. Once John Eberly even cut a section of her hair off with a yellow plastic scissors stolen from art class. This was the one time Charlie saw Joan cry actual tears. He was as bad as the others: worse, because what the others did because they felt like it, he did out of a plan, to make himself more popular. In the first and second grade he had been liked pretty well, but somewhere since then he had been dropped. There was a gang, boys and girls both, that met Saturdays – you heard them talk about it on Mondays – in Stuart Morrison's garage, and took hikes and played touch football together, and in winter sledded on Hill Street, and in spring bicycled all over Olinger and did together what else he couldn't imagine. Charlie had known the chief members since before kindergarten. But after school there seemed nothing for him to do but go home promptly and do his homework and fiddle with his Central American stamps and go to Tarzan movies alone, and on weekends nothing but beat monotonously at marbles or Monopoly or chess Darryl Johns or Marvin Auerbach, who he wouldn't have bothered at all with if they hadn't lived right in the neighborhood, they being at least a year younger and not bright for their age either. Charlie thought the gang might notice him and take him in if he backed up their policies without being asked.

In science, which 5A had in Miss Brobst's room across the hall, he sat one seat ahead of Joan and annoyed her all he could, in spite of a feeling that, both being disliked, they had something to share. One fact he discovered was, she wasn't that bright. Her marks on quizzes were always lower than his. He told her, "Cutting up all those flowers didn't do you much good. Or maybe in Baltimore they taught you everything so long ago you've forgotten it in your old age."

Charlie drew; on his tablet, where she could easily see over his shoulder, he once in a while drew a picture titled "Joan the Dope": the profile of a girl with a lean nose and sad mincemouth, the lashes of her lowered eye as black as the pencil could make them, and the hair falling, in ridiculous hooks, row after row, down through the sea-blue cross-lines clear off the bottom edge of the tablet.

March turned into spring. One of the signals was, on the high-school grounds, before the cinder track was weeded and when the softball field was still four inches of mud, Happy Lasker came with the elaborate airplane model he had wasted the winter making. It had the American star on the wingtips and a pilot painted inside the cockpit and a miniature motor that burned real gas. The buzzing, off and on all Saturday morning, collected smaller kids from Second Street down to Lynoak. Then it was always the same: Happy shoved the plane into the air, where it climbed and made a razzing noise a minute, then nose-dived and crashed and usually burned in the grass or mud. Happy's father was rich.

In the weeks since she had come, Joan's clothes had slowly grown simpler, to go with the other girls', and one day she came to school with most of her hair cut off, and the rest brushed flat around her head and brought into a little tail behind. The laughter at her was more than she had ever heard. "Ooh. Baldy-paldy!" some idiot girl had exclaimed when Joan came into the cloakroom, and the stupid words went sliding around class all morning. "Baldy-paldy from Baltimore. Why is old Baldy-paldy red in the face?" John Eberly kept making the motion of a scissors with his fingers and its juicy ticking sound with his tongue. Miss Fritz rapped her knuckles on the windowsill until she was rubbing the ache with the other hand, and finally she sent two boys to Mr. Lengel's office, delighting Charlie an enormous secret amount.

His own reaction to the haircut had been quiet: to want to draw her, changed. He had kept the other drawings folded in his desk, and one of his instincts was toward complete sets of things, Batman comics and A's and Costa Rican stamps. Halfway across the room from him, Joan held very still, afraid, it seemed, to move even a hand, her face a shamed pink. The haircut had brought out her forehead and exposed her neck and made her chin pointier and her eyes larger. Charlie felt thankful once again for having been born a boy, and having no sharp shocks, like losing your curls or starting to bleed, to make growing painful. How much girls suffer had been one of the first thoughts he had ever had.

His caricature of her was wonderful, the work of a genius.

He showed it to Stuart Morrison behind him; it was too good for him to appreciate, his dull egg eyes just flickered over it. Charlie traced it onto another piece of tablet paper, making her head completely bald. This drawing Stuart grabbed, and it was passed clear around the room.

That night he had the dream. He must have dreamed it while lying there asleep in the morning light, for it was fresh in his head when he woke. They had been in a jungle. Joan, dressed in a torn sarong, was swimming in a clear river among alligators. Somehow, as if from a tree, he was looking down, and there was a calmness in the way the slim girl and the green alligators moved, in and out, perfectly visible under the window-skin of the water. Joan's face sometimes showed the horror she was undergoing and sometimes looked numb. Her hair trailed behind and fanned when her face came toward the surface. He shouted silently with grief. Then he had rescued her; without a sense of having dipped his arms in water, he was carrying her in two arms, himself in a bathing suit, and his feet firmly fixed to the knobby back of an alligator which skimmed upstream, through the shadows of high trees and white flowers and hanging vines, like a surfboard in a movie short. They seemed to be heading toward a wooden bridge arching over the stream. He wondered how he would duck it, and the river and the jungle gave way to his bed and his room, but through the change persisted, like a pedalled note on a piano, the sweetness and pride he had felt in saving and carrying the girl.

He loved Joan Edison. The morning was rainy, and under the umbrella his mother made him take this new knowledge, repeated again and again to himself, gathered like a bell of smoke. Love had no taste, but sharpened his sense of smell so that his oilcloth coat, his rubber boots, the red-tipped bushes

31

hanging over the low walls holding back lawns all along Grand Street, even the dirt and moss in the cracks of the pavement each gave off clear odors. He would have laughed, if a wooden weight had not been placed high in his chest, near where his throat joined. He could not imagine himself laughing soon. It seemed he had reached one of those situations his Sunday-school teacher, poor Miss West with her little mustache, had been trying to prepare him for. He prayed, *Give me Joan*. With the wet weather a solemn flatness had fallen over everything; an orange bus turning at the Bend and four birds on a telephone wire seemed to have the same importance. Yet he felt firmer and lighter and felt things as edges he must whip around and channels he must rush down. If he carried her off, did rescue her from the others' cruelty, he would have defied the gang and made a new one, his own. Just Joan and he at first, then others escaping from meanness and dumbness, until his gang was stronger and Stuart Morrison's garage was empty every Saturday. Charlie would be a king, with his own touch-football game. Everyone would come and plead with him for mercy.

His first step was to tell all those in the cloakroom he loved Joan Edison now. They cared less than he had expected, considering how she was hated. He had more or less expected to have to fight with his fists. Hardly anybody gathered to hear the dream he had pictured himself telling everybody. Anyway, that morning it would go around the class that he had said he loved her, and though this was what he wanted, to in a way open a space between him and Joan, it felt funny nevertheless, and he stuttered when Miss Fritz had him go to the blackboard to explain something.

At lunch, he deliberately hid in the variety store until he saw her walk by. The homely girl with her he knew turned off at the next street. He waited a minute and then came out and began running to overtake Joan in the block between the street where the other girl turned down and the street where he turned up. It had stopped raining, and his rolled-up umbrella felt like a commando's bayonet. Coming up behind her, he said, "Bang. Bang."

She turned, and under her gaze, knowing she knew he loved her, he felt his face go hot and he stared down. "Why, Charlie," her voice said with her Maryland slowness, "what are you doing on this side of the street?" Carl the town cop stood in front of the elementary school to get them on the side of Grand Street where they belonged. Now Charlie would have to cross the avenue again, by himself, at the Bend, a dangerous five-spoked intersection.

"Nothing," he said, and used up the one sentence he had prepared ahead: "I like your hair the new way."

"Thank you," she said, and stopped. In Baltimore she must have had manners lessons. Her eyes looked at his, and his vision jumped back from the rims of her lower lids as if from a brink. Yet in the space she occupied there was a great fullness that lent him height, as if he were standing by a window giving on the first morning after a snow.

"But, then, I didn't mind it the old way either."

"Yes?"

A peculiar reply. Another peculiar thing was the tan beneath her skin; he had noticed before, though not so closely, how when she colored it came up a gentle dull brown more than red. Also, she wore something perfumed.

He asked, "How do you like Olinger?"

"Oh, I think it's nice."

"Nice? I guess. I guess maybe. Nice Olinger. I wouldn't know, because I've never been anywhere else."

She luckily took this as a joke and laughed. Rather than risk saying something unfunny, he began to balance the

33

umbrella by its point on one finger and, when this went well, walked backwards, shifting the balanced umbrella, its hook black against the patchy blue sky, from one palm to the other, back and forth. At the corner where they parted he got carried away and in imitating a suave sophisticated gent leaning on a cane bent the handle hopelessly. Her amazement was worth twice the price of his mother's probable scolding.

He planned to walk Joan again, and farther, after school. All through lunch he kept calculating. His father and he would repaint his bike. At the next haircut he would have his hair parted on the other side to get away from his cowlick. He would change himself totally; everyone would wonder what had happened to him. He would learn to swim, and take her to the dam.

In the afternoon the momentum of the dream wore off somewhat. Now that he kept his eyes always on her, he noticed, with a qualm of his stomach, that in passing in the afternoon from Miss Brobst's to Miss Fritz's room Joan was not alone, but chattered with others. In class, too, she whispered. So it was with more shame – such shame that he didn't believe he could ever face even his parents again – than surprise that from behind the dark pane of the variety store he saw her walk by in the company of the gang, she and Stuart Morrison throwing back their teeth and screaming and he imitating something and poor moronic John Eberly tagging behind like a thick tail. Charlie watched them walk out of sight behind a tall hedge; relief was as yet a tiny fraction of his reversed world. It came to him that what he had taken for cruelty had been love, that far from hating her everybody had loved her from the beginning, and that even the stupidest knew it weeks before he did. That she was the queen of the class and might as well not exist, for all the good he would get out of it.

# PIGEON FEATHERS

WHEN THEY MOVED TO FIRETOWN, things were upset, displaced, rearranged. A red cane-back sofa that had been the chief piece in the living room at Olinger was here banished, too big for the narrow country parlor, to the barn, and shrouded under a tarpaulin. Never again would David lie on its length all afternoon eating raisins and reading mystery novels and science fiction and P. G. Wodehouse. The blue wing chair that had stood for years in the ghostly, immaculate guest bedroom, gazing through the windows curtained with dotted swiss toward the telephone wires and horse-chestnut trees and opposite houses, was here established importantly in front of the smutty little fireplace that supplied, in those first cold April days, their only heat. As a child, David had been afraid of the guest bedroom – it was there that he, lying sick with the measles, had seen a black rod the size of a yardstick jog along at a slight slant beside the edge of the bed and vanish when he screamed – and it was disquieting to have one of the elements of its haunted atmosphere basking by the fire, in the center of the family, growing sooty with use. The books that at home had gathered dust in the case beside the piano were here hastily stacked, all out of order, in the shelves that the carpenters had built along one wall below the deep-silled windows. David, at thirteen, had been more moved than a mover; like the furniture, he had to find a new place, and on the Saturday of the second week he tried to work off some of his disorientation by arranging the books.

It was a collection obscurely depressing to him, mostly books his mother had acquired when she was young: college anthologies of Greek plays and Romantic poetry, Will Durant's *The Story of Philosophy*, a soft-leather set of Shakespeare with string bookmarks sewed to the bindings, *Green Mansions* boxed and illustrated with woodcuts, *I, the Tiger*, by Manuel Komroff, novels by names like Galsworthy and Ellen Glasgow and Irvin S. Cobb and Sinclair Lewis and "Elizabeth." The odor of faded taste made him feel the ominous gap between himself and his parents, the insulting gulf of time that existed before he was born. Suddenly he was tempted to dip into this time. From the heaps of books piled around him on the worn old floorboards, he picked up Volume II of a four-volume set of *The Outline of History*, by H. G. Wells. Once David had read *The Time Machine*; this gave him a small grip on the author. The book's red binding had faded to orange-pink on the spine. When he lifted the cover, there was a sweetish, moldy smell, and his mother's maiden name written in unfamiliar handwriting on the flyleaf – an upright, bold, yet careful signature, bearing a faint relation to the quick scrunched backslant that flowed with marvellous consistency across her shopping lists and budget accounts and Christmas cards to college friends from this same, vaguely menacing long ago.

He leafed through, pausing at drawings, done in an old-fashioned stippled style, of bas-reliefs, masks, Romans without pupils in their eyes, articles of ancient costume, fragments of pottery found in unearthed homes. He knew it would be interesting in a magazine, sandwiched between ads and jokes, but in this undiluted form history was somehow sour. The print was determinedly legible, and smug, like a lesson book. As he bent over the pages, yellow at the edges, they seemed rectangles of dusty glass through which he looked down into unreal and irrelevant worlds. He could see things sluggishly move, and an unpleasant fullness came into his throat. His mother and grandmother fussed in the kitchen; the puppy, which they had just acquired, as a watchdog in the country, was cowering, with a sporadic panicked scrabble of claws, under the dining table that in their old home had been reserved for special days but that here was used for every meal.

Then, before he could halt his eyes, David slipped into Wells's account of Jesus. He had been an obscure political agitator, a kind of hobo, in a minor colony of the Roman Empire. By an accident impossible to reconstruct, he (the small *h* horrified David) survived his own crucifixion and presumably died a few weeks later. A religion was founded on the freakish incident. The credulous imagination of the times retrospectively assigned miracles and supernatural pretensions to Jesus; a myth grew, and then a church, whose theology at most points was in direct contradiction of the simple, rather communistic teachings of the Galilean.

It was as if a stone that for months and even years had been gathering weight in the web of David's nerves snapped them and plunged through the page and a hundred layers of paper underneath. These fantastic falsehoods – plainly untrue: churches stood everywhere, the entire nation was founded "under God" – did not at first frighten him; it was the fact that they had been permitted to exist in an actual human brain. This was the initial impact – that at a definite spot in time and space a brain black with the denial of Christ's divinity had been suffered to exist. The universe had not spat out this ball of tar but allowed it to continue in its blasphemy, to grow old, win honors, wear a hat, write books that, if true, collapsed everything into a jumble of horror. The world outside the deep-silled windows – a rutted lawn, a whitewashed barn, a walnut tree frothy with fresh green – seemed a haven from which David was forever sealed off. Hot washrags seemed pressed against his cheeks.

He read the account again. He tried to supply out of his ignorance objections that would defeat the complacent march of these black words, and found none. Survivals and misunderstandings more farfetched were reported daily in the papers. But none of them caused churches to be built in every town. He tried to work backwards through the churches, from their brave high fronts through their shabby, ill-attended interiors back into the events at Jerusalem, and felt himself surrounded by shifting gray shadows, centuries of history, where he knew nothing. The thread dissolved in his hands. Had Christ ever come to him, David Kern, and said, "Here. Feel the wound in My side"? No; but prayers had been answered. What prayers? He had prayed that Rudy Mohn, whom he had purposely tripped so he cracked his head on their radiator, not die, and he had not died. But for all the blood, it was just a cut; Rudy came back the same day, wearing a bandage and repeating the same teasing words. He could never have died. Again, David had prayed for two separate war-effort posters he had sent away for to arrive tomorrow, and though they did not, they did arrive, some days later, together, popping through the clacking letter slot like a rebuke from God's mouth: *I answer your prayers in My way, in My time.* After that, he had made his prayers less definite, less susceptible of being twisted into a scolding. But what a tiny, ridiculous coincidence this was, after all, to throw into battle against H. G. Wells's engines of knowledge! Indeed, it proved the enemy's point: hope bases vast premises on foolish accidents, and reads a word where in fact only a scribble exists.

\* \* \*

40

His father came home. Though Saturday was a free day for him, he had been working. He taught school in Olinger and spent his free days performing, with a kind of panic, needless errands. A city boy by birth, he was frightened of the farm and seized any excuse to get away. The farm had been David's mother's birthplace; it had been her idea to buy it back. With a determination unparalleled in her life, she had gained that end, and moved them all here – her son, her husband, her mother. Granmom, in her prime, had worked these fields alongside her husband, but now she dabbled around the kitchen, her hands waggling with Parkinson's disease. She was always in the way. Strange, out in the country, amid eighty acres, they were crowded together. His father expressed his feelings of discomfort by conducting with Mother an end-less argument about organic farming. All through dusk, all through supper, it rattled on.

"Elsie, I *know*, I know from my education, the earth is nothing but chemicals. It's the only damn thing I got out of four years of college, so don't tell me it's not true."

"George, if you'd just walk out on the farm you'd know it's not true. The land has a *soul*."

"Soil, has, no, soul," he said, enunciating stiffly, as if to a very stupid class. To David he said, "You can't argue with a femme. Your mother's a real femme. That's why I married her, and now I'm suffering for it."

"*This* soil has no soul," she said, "because it's been killed with superphosphate. It's been burned bare by Boyer's tenant farmers." Boyer was the rich man they had bought the farm from. "It used to have a soul, didn't it, Mother? When you and Pop farmed it?"

"Ach, yes; I guess." Granmom was trying to bring a forkful of food to her mouth with her less severely afflicted hand. In her attempt she brought the other hand up from her lap. The crippled fingers, dull red in the orange light of the kerosene lamp in the center of the table, were welded by disease into one knobbed hook.

"Only human indi-vidu-als have souls," his father went on, in the same mincing, lifeless voice. "Because the Bible tells us so." Done eating, he crossed his legs and dug into his ear with a match; to get at the thing inside his head he tucked in his chin, and his voice came out low-pitched at David. "When God made your mother, He made a real femme."

"George, don't you read the papers? Don't you know that between the chemical fertilizers and the bug sprays we'll all be dead in ten years? Heart attacks are killing every man in the country over forty-five."

He sighed wearily; the yellow skin of his eyelids wrinkled as he hurt himself with the match. "There's no connection," he stated, spacing his words with pained patience, "between the heart and chemical fertilizers. It's alcohol that's doing it. Alcohol and milk. There is too much cholesterol in the tissues of the American heart. Don't tell me about chemistry, Elsie; I majored in the damn stuff for four years."

"Yes, and I majored in philosophy and I'm not a penny wiser. Mother, put your waggler *away*!" The old woman started, and the food dropped from her fork. For some reason, the sight of her bad hand at the table cruelly irritated her daughter. Granmom's eyes widened behind her cockeyed spectacles. Circles of silver as fine as thread, the frames clung to the red notches they had carved over the years into her little white beak. In the orange flicker of the kerosene lamp, her dazed misery seemed infernal. David's mother began, without noise, to cry. His father did not seem to have eyes at all, just jaundiced sockets of wrinkled skin. The steam of food clouded the scene, which was grim but familiar and distracted David from the formless dread that worked, sticky and sore, within him, like a too-large wound trying to heal.

He had to go to the bathroom. He took a flashlight down through the wet grass to the outhouse. For once, his fear of spiders there felt trivial. He set the flashlight, burning, beside him, and an insect alighted on its lens, a tiny insect, a mosquito or flea, made so fine that the weak light projected its X-ray onto the wall boards: the faint rim of its wings, the blurred strokes, magnified, of its long hinged legs, the dark cone at the heart of its anatomy. The tremor must be its heart beating.

Without warning, David was visited by an exact vision of death: a long hole in the ground, no wider than your body, down which you are drawn while the white faces above recede. You try to reach them but your arms are pinned. Shovels pour dirt into your face. There you will be forever, in an upright position, blind and silent, and in time no one will remember you, and you will never be called by any angel. As strata of rock shift, your fingers elongate, and your teeth are distended sideways in a great underground grimace indistinguishable from a strip of chalk. And the earth tumbles on, and the sun expires, and unaltering darkness reigns where once there were stars.

Sweat broke out on his back. His mind seemed to rebound off a solidness. Such extinction was not another threat, a graver sort of danger, a kind of pain; it was qualitatively different. It was not even a conception that could be voluntarily pictured; it entered him from outside. His protesting nerves swarmed on its surface like lichen on a meteor. The skin of his chest was soaked with the effort of rejection. At the same time that the fear was dense and internal, it was dense and all around him; a tide of clay had swept up to the stars; space was crushed into a mass. When he stood up, automatically hunching his shoulders to keep his head away from the spiderwebs, it was with a numb sense of being cramped between two huge, rigid masses. That he had even this small freedom to move surprised him. In the narrow shelter of that rank shack, adjusting his pants, he felt – his first spark of comfort – too small to be crushed.

But in the open, as the beam of the flashlight skidded with frightened quickness across the remote surfaces of the barn and the grape arbor and the giant pine that stood by the path to the woods, the terror descended. He raced up through the clinging grass pursued, not by one of the wild animals the woods might hold, or one of the goblins his superstitious grandmother had communicated to his childhood, but by spectres out of science fiction, where gigantic cinder moons fill half the turquoise sky. As David ran, a gray planet rolled inches behind his neck. If he looked back, he would be buried. And in the momentum of his terror, hideous possibilities – the dilation of the sun, the triumph of the insects, the crabs on the shore in *The Time Machine* – wheeled out of the vacuum of make-believe and added their weight to his impending oblivion.

He wrenched the door open; the lamps within the house flared. The wicks burning here and there seemed to mirror one another. His mother was washing the dishes in a little pan of heated pump-water; Granmom hovered near her elbow. In the living room – the downstairs of the little square house was two long rooms – his father sat in front of the black fireplace restlessly folding and unfolding a newspaper as he sustained his half of the argument. "Nitrogen, phosphorus, potash: these are the three replaceable constituents of the soil. One crop of corn carries away hundreds of pounds of" – he dropped the paper into his lap and ticked them off on three fingers – "nitrogen, phosphorus, potash."

"Boyer didn't grow corn."

"*Any* crop, Elsie. The human animal –"

"You're killing the *earth*worms, George!"

"The human animal, after thousands and *thou*sands of years, learned methods whereby the chemical balance of the soil may be maintained. Don't carry me back to the Dark Ages."

"When we moved to Olinger the ground in the garden was like slate. Just one summer of my cousin's chicken dung and the earthworms came back."

"I'm sure the Dark Ages were a fine place to the poor devils born in them, but I don't want to go there. They give me the creeps." Daddy stared into the cold pit of the fireplace and clung to the rolled newspaper in his lap as if it alone were keeping him from slipping backwards and down, down.

Mother came into the doorway brandishing a fistful of wet forks. "And thanks to your DDT there soon won't be a bee left in the country. When I was a girl here you could eat a peach without washing it."

"It's primitive, Elsie. It's Dark Age stuff."

"Oh, what do *you* know about the Dark Ages?"

"I know I don't want to go back to them."

David took from the shelf, where he had placed it this afternoon, the great unabridged Webster's Dictionary that his grandfather had owned. He turned the big thin pages, floppy as cloth, to the entry he wanted, and read

soul . . . 1. An entity conceived as the essence, substance, animating principle, or actuating cause of life, or of the individual life, esp. of life manifested in psychical activities; the vehicle of individual existence, separate in nature from the body and usually held to be separable in existence.

The definition went on, into Greek and Egyptian conceptions, but David stopped short on the treacherous edge of antiquity. He needed to read no further. The careful overlapping words shingled a temporary shelter for him. "Usually held to be separable in existence" – what could be fairer, more judicious, surer?

His father was saying, "The modern farmer can't go around sweeping up after his cows. The poor devil has thousands and *thou*sands of acres on his hands. Your modern farmer uses a scientifically arrived-at mixture, like five-ten-five, or six-twelve-six, or *three*-twelve-six, and spreads it on with this wonderful modern machinery which of course we can't afford. Your modern farmer can't *afford* medieval methods."

Mother was quiet in the kitchen; her silence radiated waves of anger.

"No, now, Elsie: don't play the femme with me. Let's discuss this calmly like two rational twentieth-century people. Your organic-farming nuts aren't attacking five-ten-five; they're attacking the chemical-fertilizer crooks. The monster firms."

A cup clinked in the kitchen. Mother's anger touched David's face; his cheeks burned guiltily. Just by staying in the living room he associated himself with his father. She appeared in the doorway with red hands and tears in her eyes, and said to the two of them, "I knew you didn't want to come here but I didn't know you'd torment me like this. You talked Pop into his grave and now you'll kill me. Go ahead, George, more power to you; at least I'll be buried in good ground." She tried to turn and met an obstacle and screamed, "Mother, stop hanging on my *back*! Why don't you go to *bed*?"

"Let's all go to bed," David's father said, rising from the blue wing chair and slapping his thigh with a newspaper.

"This reminds me of death." It was a phrase of his that David had heard so often he never considered its sense.

Upstairs, he seemed to be lifted above his fears. The sheets on his bed were clean. Granmom had ironed them with a pair of flatirons saved from the Olinger attic; she plucked them hot off the stove alternately, with a wooden handle called a goose. It was a wonder, to see how she managed. In the next room, his parents grunted peaceably; they seemed to take their quarrels less seriously than he did. They made comfortable scratching noises as they carried a little lamp back and forth. Their door was open a crack, so he saw the light shift and swing. Surely there would be, in the last five minutes, in the last second, a crack of light, showing the door from the dark room to another, full of light. Thinking of it this vividly frightened him. His own dying, in a specific bed in a specific room, specific walls mottled with a particular wallpaper, the dry whistle of his breathing, the murmuring doctors, the dutiful relatives going in and out, but for him no way out but down, into that hole. *Never walk again, never touch a doorknob again.* A whisper, and his parents' light was blown out. David prayed to be reassured. Though the experiment frightened him, he lifted his hands high into the darkness above his face and begged Christ to touch them. Not hard or long: the faintest, quickest grip would be final for a lifetime. His hands waited in the air, itself a substance, which seemed to move through his fingers; or was it the pressure of his pulse? He returned his hands to beneath the covers, uncertain if they had been touched or not. For would not Christ's touch *be* infinitely gentle?

Through all the eddies of its aftermath, David clung to this thought about his revelation of extinction: that there, in the outhouse, he had struck a solid something qualitatively different, a base terror dense enough to support any height of construction. All he needed was a little help; a word, a gesture, a nod of certainty, and he would be sealed in, safe. The reassurance from the dictionary had melted in the night. Today was Sunday, a hot fair day. Across a mile of clear air the church bells called, *Celebrate, celebrate*. Only Daddy went. He put on a coat over his rolled-up shirtsleeves and got into the little old black Plymouth parked by the barn and went off, with the same pained hurried grimness of all his actions. His churning wheels, as he shifted too hastily into second, raised plumes of red dust on the dirt road. Mother walked to the far field, to see what bushes needed cutting. David, though he usually preferred to stay in the house, went with her. The puppy followed at a distance, whining as it picked its way through the stubble but floundering off timidly if one of them went back to pick it up and carry it. When they reached the crest of the far field, his mother asked, "David, what's troubling you?"

"Nothing. Why?"

She looked at him sharply. The greening woods cross-hatched the space beyond her half-gray hair. Then she showed him her profile, and gestured toward the house, which they had left a half-mile behind them. "See how it sits in the land? They don't know how to build with the land any more. Pop always said the foundations were set with the compass. We must get a compass and see. It's supposed to face due south; but south feels a little more *that* way to me." From the side, as she said these things, she seemed handsome and young. The smooth sweep of her hair over her ear had a calm that made her feel foreign to him. He had never regarded his parents as consolers of his troubles; from the beginning they had seemed to have more troubles than he. Their frailty had flattered him into an illusion of strength;

so now on this high clear ridge he jealously guarded the menace all around them, blowing like an invisible breeze – the possibility of all this wide scenery's sinking into everlasting darkness. The strange fact that, though she came to look at the brush, she carried no clippers, for she had a fixed prejudice against working on Sundays, was the only comfort he allowed her to offer.

As they walked back, the puppy whimpering after them, the rising dust behind a distant line of trees announced that Daddy was speeding home from church. When they reached the house he was there. He had brought back the Sunday paper and the vehement remark, "Dobson's too intelligent for these farmers. They just sit there with their mouths open and don't hear a thing the poor devil's saying."

"What makes you think farmers are unintelligent? This country was made by farmers. George Washington was a farmer."

"They are, Elsie. They are unintelligent. George Washington's dead. In this day and age only the misfits stay on the farm. The lame, the halt, the blind. The morons with one arm. Human garbage. They remind me of death, sitting there with their mouths open."

"My *father* was a farmer."

"He was a frustrated man, Elsie. He never knew what hit him. The poor devil meant so well, and he never knew which end was up. Your mother'll bear me out. Isn't that right, Mom? Pop never knew what hit him?"

"Ach, I guess not," the old woman quavered, and the ambiguity for the moment silenced both sides.

David hid in the funny papers and sports section until one-thirty. At two, the catechetical class met at the Firetown church. He had transferred from the catechetical class of the Lutheran church in Olinger, a humiliating comedown.

In Olinger they met on Wednesday nights, spiffy and spruce, in a very social atmosphere. Afterwards, blessed by the brick-faced minister on whose lips the word "Christ" had a pugnacious juiciness, the more daring of them went with their Bibles to a luncheonette and gossiped and smoked. Here in Firetown, the girls were dull white cows and the boys narrow-faced brown goats in old men's suits, herded on Sunday afternoons into a threadbare church basement that smelled of stale hay. Because his father had taken the car on one of his endless errands to Olinger, David walked, grateful for the open air, the lonely dirt road, and the silence. The catechetical class embarrassed him, but today he placed hope in it, as the source of the nod, the gesture, that was all he needed.

Reverend Dobson was a delicate young man with great dark eyes and small white shapely hands that flickered like protesting doves when he preached; he seemed a bit misplaced in the Lutheran ministry. This was his first call. It was a split parish; he served another rural church twelve miles away. His iridescent-green Ford, new six months ago, was spattered to the windows with red mud and rattled from bouncing on the rude back roads, where he frequently got lost, to the malicious satisfaction of some parishioners. But David's mother liked him, and, more pertinent to his success, the Haiers, the sleek family of feed merchants and tractor salesmen who dominated the Firetown church, liked him. David liked him, and felt liked in turn; sometimes in class, after some special stupidity, Dobson directed toward him out of those wide black eyes a mild look of disbelief, a look that, though flattering, was also delicately disquieting.

Catechetical instruction consisted of reading aloud from a work booklet answers to problems prepared during the week, problems like, "I am the _____, the _____, and the _____, saith the Lord." Then there was a question period in which no one ever asked any questions. Today's theme was the last third of the Apostles' Creed. When the time came for questions, David blushed and asked, "About the Resurrection of the Body – are we conscious between the time when we die and the Day of Judgment?"

Dobson blinked, and his fine small mouth pursed, suggesting that David was making difficult things more difficult. The faces of the other students went blank, as if an indiscretion had been committed.

"No, I suppose not," Reverend Dobson said.

"Well, where is our soul, then, in this gap?"

The sense grew, in the class, of a naughtiness occurring. Dobson's shy eyes watered, as if he were straining to keep up the formality of attention, and one of the girls, the fattest, simpered toward her twin, who was a little less fat. Their chairs were arranged in a rough circle. The current running around the circle panicked David. Did everybody know something he didn't know?

"I suppose you could say our souls are asleep," Dobson said.

"And then they wake up, and there is the earth like it always is, and all the people who have ever lived? Where will Heaven be?"

Anita Haier giggled. Dobson gazed at David intently, but with an awkward, puzzled flicker of forgiveness, as if there existed a secret between them that David was violating. But David knew of no secret. All he wanted was to hear Dobson repeat the words he said every Sunday morning. This he would not do. As if these words were unworthy of the conversational voice.

"David, you might think of Heaven this way: as the way in which the goodness Abraham Lincoln did lives after him."

"But is Lincoln conscious of it living on?" He blushed no

longer with embarrassment but in anger; he had walked here in good faith and was being made a fool.

"Is he conscious now? I would have to say no. But I don't think it matters." His voice had a coward's firmness; he was hostile now.

"You don't."

"Not in the eyes of God, no." The unction, the stunning impudence, of this reply sprang tears of outrage in David's eyes. He bowed them to his work book, where short words like Duty, Love, Obey, Honor were stacked in the form of a cross.

"Were there any other questions, David?" Dobson asked, more softly. The others were rustling, collecting their books.

"No." David made his voice firm, though he could not look up at the man.

"Did I answer your question fully enough?"

"Yes."

In the minister's silence the shame that should have been his crept over David: the burden and fever of being a fraud were placed upon *him*, who was innocent, and it seemed, he knew, a confession of this guilt that on the way out he was unable to face Dobson's stirred gaze, though he felt it probing the side of his head.

Anita Haier's father gave him a ride down the highway as far as the dirt road. David said he wanted to walk the rest, and figured that his offer was accepted because Mr. Haier did not want to dirty his dark new Oldsmobile with dust. This was all right; everything was all right, as long as it was clear. His indignation at being betrayed, at seeing Christianity betrayed, had hardened him. The road reflected his hardness. Pink stones thrust up through its packed surface. The April sun beat down from the center of the afternoon half of the sky; already it had some of summer's heat. Already the fringes of weeds at the edges of the road were bedraggled with dust. From the reviving grass and scruff of the fields that he walked between, insects were sending up a monotonous, automatic chant. In the distance a tiny figure in his father's coat was walking along the edge of the woods. His mother. He wondered what joy she found in such walks; to him the brown stretches of slowly rising and falling land expressed only a huge exhaustion.

Flushed with fresh air and happiness, she returned from her walk earlier than he had expected, and surprised him at his grandfather's Bible. It was a stumpy black book, the boards worn thin where the old man's fingers had held them; the spine hung by one weak hinge of fabric. David had been looking for the passage where Jesus says to the good thief on the cross, "Today shalt thou be with Me in paradise." He had never tried reading the Bible for himself before. What was so embarrassing about being caught at it was that he detested the apparatus of piety. Fusty churches, creaking hymns, ugly Sunday-school teachers and their stupid leaflets – he hated everything about them but the promise they held out, a promise that in the most perverse way, as if the homeliest crone in the kingdom were given the prince's hand, made every good and real thing, ball games and jokes and big-breasted girls, possible. He couldn't explain this to his mother. There was no time. Her solicitude was upon him.

"David, what are you doing?"

"Nothing."

"What are you doing at your grandfather's Bible?"

"Trying to read it. This is supposed to be a Christian country, isn't it?"

She sat down beside him on the green sofa, which used to

be in the sun parlor at Olinger, under the fancy mirror. A little smile still lingered on her face from the walk. "David, I wish you'd talk to me."

"What about?"

"About whatever it is that's troubling you. Your father and I have both noticed it."

"I asked Reverend Dobson about Heaven and he said it was like Abraham Lincoln's goodness living after him."

He waited for the shock to strike her. "Yes?" she said, expecting more.

"That's all."

"And why didn't you like it?"

"Well – don't you see? It amounts to saying there isn't any Heaven at all."

"I don't see that it amounts to that. What do you want Heaven to be?"

"Well, I don't know. I want it to be *some*thing. I thought he'd tell me what it was. I thought that was his job." He was becoming angry, sensing her surprise. She had assumed that Heaven had faded from his head years ago. She had imagined that he had already entered, in the secrecy of silence, the conspiracy that he now knew to be all around him.

"David," she asked gently, "don't you ever want to rest?"

"No. Not forever."

"David, you're so young. When you get older, you'll feel differently."

"Grandpa didn't. Look how tattered this book is."

"I never understood your grandfather."

"Well, I don't understand ministers who say it's like Lincoln's goodness going on and on. Suppose you're not Lincoln?"

"I think Reverend Dobson made a mistake. You must try to forgive him."

"It's not a *question* of his making a mistake! It's a question of dying and never moving or seeing or hearing anything ever again."

"But" – in exasperation – "darling, it's so *greedy* of you to want more. When God has given us this wonderful April day, and given us this farm, and you have your whole life ahead of you –"

"You think, then, that there is a God?"

"Of course I do" – with deep relief, that smoothed her features into a reposeful oval. He had risen in his unease; he was afraid she would reach out and touch him.

"He made everything? You feel that?"

"Yes."

"Then who made Him?"

"Why, Man. Man." The happiness of this answer lit up her face radiantly, until she saw his gesture of disgust. She was so simple, so illogical; such a femme.

"Well, that amounts to saying He doesn't exist."

Her hand reached for his wrist but he backed away. "David, it's a mystery. A miracle. It's a miracle more beautiful than any Reverend Dobson could have told you about. You don't say houses don't exist because Man made them."

"No. God has to be different."

"But, David, you have the *evidence*. Look out the window at the sun; at the fields."

"Mother, good grief. Don't you see" – he rasped away the roughness in his throat – "if when we die there's nothing, all your sun and fields and whatnot are all, ah, *horror*? It's just an ocean of horror."

"But, David, it's not. It's so clearly not that." And she made an urgent, opening gesture with her hands that expressed a willingness to receive his helplessness; all her grace and mater- nal nurturing were gathered into a passive intensity that intensely repelled him. He would not be wooed away from the truth. *I am the Way, the Truth* ...

"No," he told her. "Just let me alone."

He found his tennis ball behind the piano and went outside to throw it against the side of the house. There was a patch high up where the brown stucco laid over the sandstone masonry was crumbling away; he kept trying with the tennis ball to chip more pieces off. It was difficult, aiming up; the ball kept falling short.

Superimposed upon his deep ache was a smaller but more immediate worry – that he had hurt his mother. He heard his father's car rattling on the straightaway, and went into the house, to make peace before he arrived. To his relief, she was not giving off the stifling damp heat of her anger, but instead was cool, decisive, maternal. She handed him an old green book, her college text of Plato.

"I want you to read the Parable of the Cave," she said.

"All right," he said, though he knew it would do no good. Some story by a dead Greek just vague enough to please her. "Don't worry about it, Mother."

"I *am* worried. Honestly, David, I'm sure there will be something for us. As you get older, these things seem to matter a great deal less."

"That may be. It's a dismal thought, though."

His father bumped at the door. The locks and jambs stuck here. But before Granmom could totter to the latch and let him in, he had knocked it open. He had been in Olinger dithering with track-meet tickets. Although Mother usually kept her talks with David a secret between them, she called instantly, "George, David is worried about death!"

Daddy came to the doorway of the living room, his shirt pocket bristling with pencils, holding in one hand a pint box of melting ice cream and in the other the knife with which he was about to divide it into four sections, their Sunday treat. "Is the kid worried about death? Don't give it a thought, David. I'll be lucky if I live till tomorrow, and I'm not worried. If they'd taken a buckshot gun and shot me in the cradle I'd be better off. The *world*'d be better off. Hell, I think death is a wonderful thing. I look forward to it. Get the garbage out of the way. If I had the man here who invented death, I'd pin a medal on him."

"Hush, George. You'll frighten the child worse than he is."

This was not true; he never frightened David. There was no harm in his father, no harm at all. Indeed, in the man's lively self-disgust the boy felt a kind of ally. A distant ally. He saw his position with a certain strategic coldness. Nowhere in the world of other people would he find the hint, the nod, he needed to begin to build his fortress against death. They none of them believed. He was alone. In that deep hole.

In the months that followed, his position changed little. School was some comfort. All those sexy, perfumed people, wisecracking, chewing gum, all of them doomed to die, and none of them noticing. In their company David felt that they would carry him along into the bright, cheap paradise reserved for them. In any crowd, the fear ebbed a little; he had reasoned that somewhere in the world there must exist a few people who believed what was necessary, and the larger the crowd, the greater the chance that he was near such a soul, within calling distance, if only he was not too ignorant, too ill-equipped, to spot him. The sight of clergymen cheered him; whatever they themselves thought, their collars were still a sign that somewhere, at some time, someone had recognized that we cannot, *cannot*, submit to death. The sermon topics posted outside churches, the flip, hurried pieties of disc jockeys, the cartoons in magazines showing angels or devils – on such scraps he kept alive the possibility of hope.

For the rest, he tried to drown his hopelessness in clatter and jostle. The pinball machine at the luncheonette was a merciful distraction; as he bent over its buzzing, flashing board of flippers and cushions, the weight and constriction in his chest lightened and loosened. He was grateful for all the time his father wasted in Olinger. Every delay postponed the moment when they must ride together down the dirt road into the heart of the dark farmland, where the only light was the kerosene lamp waiting on the dining-room table, a light that drowned their food in shadow and made it sinister.

He lost his appetite for reading. He was afraid of being ambushed again. In mystery novels people died like dolls being discarded; in science fiction immensities of space and time conspired to annihilate the human beings; and even in P. G. Wodehouse there was a threat, a bland mockery that acquired bite in the comic figures of futile clergymen. All gaiety seemed minced out on the skin of a void. All quiet hours seemed invitations to dread.

Even on weekends, he and his father contrived to escape the farm; and when, some Saturdays, they did stay home, it was to do something destructive – tear down an old henhouse or set huge brush fires that threatened, while Mother shouted and flapped her arms, to spread to the woods. Whenever his father worked, it was with rapt violence; when he chopped kindling, fragments of the old henhouse boards flew like shrapnel and the ax-head was always within a quarter of an inch of flying off the handle. He was exhilarating to watch, sweating and swearing and sucking bits of saliva back into his mouth.

School stopped. His father took the car in the opposite direction, to a highway construction job where he had been hired for the summer as a timekeeper, and David was stranded in the middle of acres of heat and greenery and blowing pollen and the strange, mechanical humming that lay invisibly in the weeds and alfalfa and dry orchard grass.

For his fourteenth birthday his parents gave him, with jokes about him being a hillbilly now, a Remington .22. It was somewhat like a pinball machine to take it out to the old kiln in the woods where they dumped their trash, and set up tin cans on the kiln's sandstone shoulder and shoot them off one by one. He'd take the puppy, who had grown long legs and a rich coat of reddish fur – he was part chow. Copper hated the gun but loved the boy enough to accompany him. When the flat, acrid crack rang out, he would race in terrified circles that would tighten and tighten until they brought him, shivering, against David's legs. Depending upon his mood, David would shoot again or drop to his knees and comfort the dog. Giving this comfort returned some comfort to him. The dog's ears, laid flat against his skull in fear, were folded so intricately, so – he groped for the concept – *surely*. Where the dull-studded collar made the fur stand up, each hair showed a root of soft white under the length, black-tipped, of the metal color that had lent the dog its name. In his agitation Copper panted through nostrils that were elegant slits, like two healed cuts, or like the keyholes of a dainty lock of black, grained wood. His whole whorling, knotted, jointed body was a wealth of such embellishments. And in the smell of the dog's hair David seemed to descend through many finely differentiated layers of earth: mulch, soil, sand, clay, and the glittering mineral base.

But when he returned to the house, and saw the books arranged on the low shelves, fear dully returned. The four adamant volumes of Wells like four thin bricks, the green

Plato that had puzzled him with its dialogue form and hard-to-picture shadow show, the dead Galsworthy and "Elizabeth," Grandpa's mammoth dictionary, Grandpa's old Bible, the limp-covered Bible that he himself had received on becoming confirmed a member of the Firetown Lutheran Church – at the sight of these, the memory of his fear reawakened and came around him. He had grown stiff and stupid in its embrace. His parents tried to think of ways to entertain him.

"David, I have a job for you to do," his mother said one evening at the table.

"What?"

"If you're going to take that tone perhaps we'd better not talk."

"What tone? I didn't take any tone."

"Your grandmother thinks there are too many pigeons in the barn."

"Why?" David turned to look at his grandmother, but she sat there staring at the burning lamp with her usual expression of bewilderment. Her irises were pale discs of crazed crystal.

Mother shouted, "Mom, he wants to know why!"

Granmom made a jerky, irritable motion with her bad hand, as if generating the force for utterance, and said, "They foul the furniture."

"That's right," Mother said. "She's afraid for that old Olinger furniture that we'll never use. David, she's been after me for a month about those poor pigeons. She wants you to shoot them."

"I don't want to kill anything especially," David said.

Daddy said, "The kid's like you are, Elsie. He's too good for this world. Kill or be killed, that's my motto."

60

His mother said loudly, "Mother, he doesn't want to do it."

"Not?" The old lady's eyes distended as if in alarm, and her claw descended slowly to her lap.

"Oh, I'll do it, I'll do it tomorrow," David snapped, and a pleasant crisp taste entered his mouth with the decision.

"And I had thought, when Boyer's men made the hay, it would be better if the barn doesn't look like a rookery," his mother added needlessly.

A barn, in day, is a small night. The splinters of light between the dry shingles pierce the high roof like stars, and the rafters and crossbeams and built-in ladders seem, until your eyes adjust, as mysterious as the branches of a haunted forest. David entered silently, the gun in one hand. Copper whined desperately at the door, too frightened to come in with the gun yet unwilling to leave the boy. David stealthily turned, said "Go away," shut the door on the dog, and slipped the bolt across. It was a door within a door; the double door for wagons and tractors was as high and wide as the face of a house.

The smell of old straw scratched his sinuses. The red sofa, half hidden under its white-splotched tarpaulin, seemed assimilated into this smell, sunk in it, buried. The mouths of empty bins gaped like caves. Rusty oddments of farming – coils of baling wire, some spare tines for a harrow, a handleless shovel – hung on nails driven here and there in the thick wood. He stood stock-still a minute; it took a while to separate the cooing of the pigeons from the rustling in his ears. When he had focused on the cooing, it flooded the vast interior with its throaty, bubbling outpour: there seemed no other sound. They were up behind the beams. What light there was leaked through the shingles and the dirty glass windows at the far end and the small round holes, about as big as basketballs, high on the opposite stone side walls, under the ridge of the roof.

A pigeon appeared in one of these holes, on the side toward the house. It flew in, with a battering of wings, from the outside, and waited there, silhouetted against its pinched bit of sky, preening and cooing in a throbbing, thrilled, tentative way. David tiptoed four steps to the side, rested his gun against the lowest rung of a ladder pegged between two upright beams, and lowered the gunsight into the bird's tiny, jauntily cocked head. The slap of the report seemed to come off the stone wall behind him, and the pigeon did not fall. Neither did it fly. Instead it stuck in the round hole, pirouetting rapidly and nodding its head as if in frantic agreement. David shot the bolt back and forth and had aimed again before the spent cartridge had stopped jingling on the boards by his feet. He eased the tip of the sight a little lower, into the bird's breast, and took care to squeeze the trigger with perfect evenness. The slow contraction of his hand abruptly sprang the bullet; for a half-second there was doubt, and then the pigeon fell like a handful of rags, skimming down the barn wall into the layer of straw that coated the floor of the mow on this side.

Now others shook loose from the rafters, and whirled in the dim air with a great blurred hurtle of feathers and noise. They would go for the hole; he fixed his sight on the little moon of blue, and when a pigeon came to it, shot him as he was walking the twenty inches of stone that would have carried him into the open air. This pigeon lay down in that tunnel of stone, unable to fall either one way or the other, although he was alive enough to lift one wing and cloud the light. The wing would sink back, and he would suddenly lift it again, the feathers flaring. His body blocked that exit. David raced to the other side of the barn's main aisle, where a similar ladder was symmetrically placed, and rested his gun on the same rung. Three birds came together to this hole; he got one, and two got through. The rest resettled in the rafters.

There was a shallow triangular space behind the cross-beams supporting the roof. It was here they roosted and hid. But either the space was too small, or they were curious, for now that his eyes were at home in the dusty gloom David could see little dabs of gray popping in and out. The cooing was shriller now; its apprehensive tremolo made the whole volume of air seem liquid. He noticed one little smudge of a head that was especially persistent in peeking out; he marked the place, and fixed his gun on it, and when the head appeared again, had his finger tightened in advance on the trigger. A parcel of fluff slipped off the beam and fell the barn's height onto a canvas covering some Olinger furniture, and where its head had peeked out there was a fresh prick of light in the shingles.

Standing in the center of the floor, fully master now, disdaining to steady the barrel with anything but his arm, he killed two more that way. Out of the shadowy ragged infinity of the vast barn roof these impudent things dared to thrust their heads, presumed to dirty its starred silence with their filthy timorous life, and he cut them off, tucked them back neatly into the silence. He felt like a creator; these little smudges and flickers that he was clever to see and even cleverer to hit in the dim recesses of the rafters – out of each of them he was making a full bird. A tiny peek, probe, dab of life, when he hit it blossomed into a dead enemy, falling with good, final weight.

The imperfection of the second pigeon he had shot, who was still lifting his wing now and then up in the round hole, nagged him. He put a new clip into the stock. Hugging the gun against his body, he climbed the ladder. The barrel sight scratched his ear; he had a sharp, garish vision, like a color slide, of shooting himself and being found tumbled on the barn floor among his prey. He locked his arm around the top rung – a fragile, gnawed rod braced between uprights – and shot into the bird's body from a flat angle. The wing folded, but the impact did not, as he had hoped, push the bird out of the hole. He fired again, and again, and still the little body, lighter than air when alive, was too heavy to budge from its high grave. From up here he could see green trees and a brown corner of the house through the hole. Clammy with the cobwebs that gathered between the rungs, he pumped a full clip of eight bullets into the stubborn shadow, with no success. He climbed down, and was struck by the silence in the barn. The remaining pigeons must have escaped out the other hole. That was all right; he was tired of it.

He stepped with his rifle into the light. His mother was coming to meet him, and it tickled him to see her shy away from the carelessly held gun. "You took a chip out of the house," she said. "What were those last shots about?"

"One of them died up in that little round hole and I was trying to shoot it down."

"Copper's hiding behind the piano and won't come out. I had to leave him."

"Well, don't blame me. *I* didn't want to shoot the poor devils."

"Don't smirk. You look like your father. How many did you get?"

"Six."

She went into the barn, and he followed. She listened to the silence. Her hair was scraggly, perhaps from tussling with the dog. "I don't suppose the others will be back," she

64

said wearily. "Indeed, I don't know why I let Mother talk me into it. Their cooing was such a comforting noise." She began to gather up the dead pigeons. Though he didn't want to touch them, David went into the mow and picked up by its tepid, horny, coral-colored feet the first bird he had killed. Its wings unfolded disconcertingly, as if the creature had been held together by threads that now were slit. It did not weigh much. He retrieved the one on the other side of the barn; his mother got the three in the middle and led the way across the road to the little south-facing slope of land that went down toward the foundations of the vanished tobacco shed. The ground was too steep to plant and mow; wild strawberries grew in the tangled grass. She put her burden down and said, "We'll have to bury them. The dog will go wild."

He put his two down on her three; the slick feathers let the bodies slide liquidly on one another. David asked, "Shall I get you the shovel?"

"Get it for yourself; *you* bury them. They're your kill. And be sure to make the hole deep enough so Copper won't dig them up." While he went to the tool shed for the shovel, she went into the house. Unlike his usual mother, she did not look up, either at the orchard to the right of her or at the meadow on her left, but instead held her head rigidly, tilted a little, as if listening to the ground.

He dug the hole, in a spot where there were no strawberry plants, before he studied the pigeons. He had never seen a bird this close before. The feathers were more wonderful than dog's hair, for each filament was shaped within the shape of the feather, and the feathers in turn were trimmed to fit a pattern that flowed without error across the bird's body. He lost himself in the geometrical tides as the feathers now broadened and stiffened to make an edge for flight, now softened and constricted to cup warmth around the mute flesh. And across the surface of the infinitely adjusted yet somehow effortless mechanics of the feathers played idle designs of color, no two alike, designs executed, it seemed, in a controlled rapture, with a joy that hung level in the air above and behind him. Yet these birds bred in the millions and were exterminated as pests. Into the fragrant open earth he dropped one broadly banded in slate shades of blue, and on top of it another, mottled all over in rhythms of lilac and gray. The next was almost wholly white, but for a salmon glaze at its throat. As he fitted the last two, still pliant, on the top, and stood up, crusty coverings were lifted from him, and with a feminine, slipping sensation along his nerves that seemed to give the air hands, he was robed in this certainty: that the God who had lavished such craft upon these worthless birds would not destroy His whole Creation by refusing to let David live forever.

# FRIENDS FROM
# PHILADELPHIA

IN THE MOMENT before the door was opened to him, he glimpsed her thigh below the half-drawn shade. Thelma was home, then. She was wearing the Camp Winniwoho T-shirt and her quite short shorts.

"Why, my goodness: Janny!" she cried. She always pronounced his name, John, to rhyme with "Ann." Earlier that summer, she had visited New York City, and tried to talk the way she thought they talked there. "What on earth ever brings you to me at this odd hour?"

"Hello, Thel," he said. "I hope – I guess this is a pretty bad time." She had been plucking her eyebrows again. He wished she wouldn't do that.

Thelma extended her arm and touched her fingers to the base of John's neck. It wasn't a fond gesture, just a hostesslike one. "Now, Janny. You know that I – my mother and I – are always happy to be seeing you. Mother, who do you ever guess is here at this odd hour?"

"Don't keep John Nordholm standing there," Mrs. Lutz said. Thelma's mother was settled in the deep-red settee watching television and smoking. A coffee cup being used as an ashtray lay in her lap, and her dress was hitched so that her knees showed.

"Hello, Mrs. Lutz," John said, trying not to look at her broad, pale knees. "I really hate to bother you at this odd hour."

"I don't see anything odd about it." She took a deep-throated drag on her cigarette and exhaled through her nostrils, the way men do. "Some of the other kids were here earlier this afternoon."

"I would have come in if anybody had told me."

Thelma said, "Oh, Janny! Stop trying to make a martyr of yourself. Keep in touch, they say, if you want to keep up."

He felt his face grow hot and knew he was blushing, which made him blush all the more. Mrs. Lutz shook a wrinkled pack of Herbert Tareytons at him. "Smoke?" she said.

"I guess not, thanks a lot."

"You've stopped? It's a bad habit. I wish I had stopped at your age. I'm not sure I'd even *begun* at your age."

"No, it's just that I have to go home soon, and my mother would smell the smoke on my breath. She can smell it even through chewing gum."

"Why must you go home soon?" Thelma asked.

Mrs. Lutz sniffled. "I have sinus. I can't even smell the flowers in the garden or the food on the table any more. Let the kids smoke if they want, if it makes them feel better. I don't care. My Thelma, she can smoke right in her own home, her own living room, if she wants to. But she doesn't seem to have the taste for it. I'm just as glad, to tell the truth."

John hated interrupting, but it was close to five-thirty. "I have a problem," he said.

"A problem – how gruesome," Thelma said. "And here I thought, Mother, I was being favored with a social call."

"Don't talk like that," Mrs. Lutz said.

"It's sort of complex," John began.

"Talk like what, Mother? Talk like what?"

"Then let me turn this off," Mrs. Lutz said, snapping the right knob on the television set.

"Oh, Mother, and I was listening to it!" Thelma toppled into a chair, her legs flashing. When she pouted, John thought, she was delicious.

70

Mrs. Lutz had set herself to give sympathy. Her lap was broadened and her hands were laid palm upward in it.

"It's not much of a problem," John assured her. "But we're having some people to dinner from Philadelphia." He turned to Thelma and added, "If anything is going on tonight, I can't get out."

"Life is just too, too full of disappointments," Thelma said.

"Look, is there?"

"Too, too full," Thelma said.

Mrs. Lutz made fluttery motions out of her lap. "These Philadelphia people."

John said, "Maybe I shouldn't bother you about this." He waited, but she just looked more and more patient, so he went on. "My mother wants to give them wine, and my father isn't home from school yet. He might not get home before the liquor store closes. It's at six, isn't it? My mother's busy cleaning the house, so I walked in."

"She made you walk the whole mile? Poor thing, can't you drive?" Mrs. Lutz asked.

"*Sure* I can drive. But I'm not sixteen yet."

"You look a lot taller than fifteen."

John looked at Thelma to see how she took that one, but Thelma was pretending to read a rented novel wrapped in cellophane.

"I walked all the way to the liquor store," John told Mrs. Lutz, "but they wouldn't give me anything without written permission. It was a new man."

"Your sorrow has rent me in twain," Thelma said, as if she was reading it from the book.

"Pay no attention, John," Mrs. Lutz said. "Frank will be home any second. Why not wait until he comes and let him run down with you for a bottle?"

"That sounds wonderful. Thanks an awful lot, really."

Mrs. Lutz's hand descended upon the television knob. Some smiling man was playing the piano. John didn't know who he was; there wasn't any television at his house. They watched in silence until Mr. Lutz thumped on the porch outside. The empty milk bottles tinkled, as if they had been nudged. "Now, don't be surprised if he has a bit of a load on," Mrs. Lutz said.

Actually, he didn't act at all drunk. He was like a happy husband in the movies. He called Thelma his little pookie-pie and kissed her on the forehead; then he called his wife his big pookie-pie and kissed her on the mouth. Then he solemnly shook John's hand and told him how very, very happy he was to see him here and asked after his parents. "Is that goon still on television?" he said finally.

"Daddy, please pay attention to somebody else," Thelma said, turning off the television set. "Janny wants to talk to you."

"And *I* want to talk to *Johnny*," Thelma's father said. He spread his arms suddenly, clenching and unclenching his fists. He was a big man, with shaved gray hair above his ears, which were small and flat to his head. John couldn't think of the word to begin.

Mrs. Lutz explained the errand. When she was through, Mr. Lutz said, "People from Philadelphia. I bet their name isn't William L. Trexler, is it?"

"No. I forget their name, but it's not that. The man is an engineer. The woman went to college with my mother."

"Oh. College people. Then we must get them something very, very nice, I should say."

"Daddy," Thelma said. "*Please*. The store will close."

"Tessie, you hear John. People from college. People with diplomas. And it is very nearly closing time, and who isn't on their way?" He took John's shoulder in one hand and

72

Thelma's arm in the other and hustled them through the door. "We'll be back in one minute, Mamma," he said.

"Drive carefully," Mrs. Lutz said from the shadowed porch.

Mr. Lutz drove a huge blue Buick. "I never went to college," he said, "yet I buy a new car whenever I want." His tone wasn't nasty, but soft and full of wonder.

"Oh, Daddy, not *this* again," Thelma said, shaking her head at John, so he could understand what all she had to go through. When she looks like that, John thought, I could bite her lip until it bleeds.

"Ever driven this kind of car, John?" Mr. Lutz asked.

"No. The only thing I can drive is my parents' Plymouth, and that not very well."

"What year car is it?"

"I don't know exactly." John knew perfectly well it was a 1940 model, bought second-hand after the war. "It has a gear shift. This is automatic, isn't it?"

"Automatic shift, fluid transmission, directional lights, the works," Mr. Lutz said. "Now, isn't it funny, John? Here is your father, an educated man, with an old Plymouth, yet at the same time I, who never read more than ten, twenty books in my life ... It doesn't seem as if there's justice." He slapped the fender, bent over to get into the car, straightened up abruptly, and said, "Do you want to drive it?"

Thelma said, "Daddy's asking you something."

"I don't know how," John said.

"It's very easy to learn, very easy. You just slide in there — come on, it's getting late." John got in on the driver's side. He peered out of the windshield. It was a wider car than the Plymouth; the hood looked wide as a boat.

Mr. Lutz asked him to grip the little lever behind the steering wheel. "You pull it toward you like *that*, that's it,

73

and fit it into one of these notches. 'P' stands for 'park' –
for when you're not going anywhere. 'N,' that's 'neutral,'
like on the car you have, I hardly ever use it, 'D' means
'drive' – just put it in there and the car does all the work for
you. You are using that one ninety-nine per cent of the time.
'L' is 'low,' for very steep hills, going up or down. And 'R'
stands for – what?"

"Reverse," John said.

"Very, very good. Tessie, he's a smart boy. He'll never own
a new car. And when you put them all together, you can
remember their order by the sentence 'Paint No Dimes Light
Red.' I thought that up when I was teaching my oldest girl
how to drive."

"Paint No Dimes Light Red," John said.

"Excellent. Now, let's go." He reached over and put the
car key in the ignition lock, his other keys dangling.

A bubble was developing in John's stomach. "What gear
do you want it in to start?" he asked Mr. Lutz.

Mr. Lutz must not have heard him, because all he said was
"Let's go" again, and he drummed on the dashboard with his
fingertips. They were thick, square, furry fingers.

Thelma leaned up from the back seat. Her cheek almost
touched John's ear. She whispered, "Put it at 'D.' "

He did, then he looked for the starter. "How does he start
it?" he asked Thelma.

"I never watch him," she said. "There was a button in the
last car, but I don't see it in this one."

"Push on the pedal," Mr. Lutz sang, staring straight ahead
and smiling, "and away we go. And ah, ah, *waay* we go."

"Just step on the gas," Thelma suggested. John pushed
down firmly, to keep his leg from trembling. The motor
roared and the car bounded away from the curb. Within a
block, though, he could manage the car pretty well.

"It rides like a boat on smooth water," he told his two passengers. The simile pleased him.

Mr. Lutz squinted ahead. "Like a what?"

"Like a boat."

"Don't go so fast," Thelma said.

"The motor's so quiet," John explained. "Like a sleeping cat."

Without warning, a truck pulled out of Pearl Street. Mr. Lutz, trying to brake, stamped his foot on the empty floor in front of him. John could hardly keep from laughing. "I see him," he said, easing his speed so that the truck had just enough room to make its turn. "Those trucks think they own the road," he said. He let one hand slide away from the steering wheel. One-handed, he whipped around a bus. "What'll she do on the open road?"

"That's a good question, John," Mr. Lutz said. "And I don't know the answer. Ninety, maybe."

"The speedometer goes up to a hundred and ten." Another pause – nobody seemed to be talking. John said, "Hell. A baby could drive one of these."

"For instance, you," Thelma said. That meant she had noticed how well he was driving.

There were a lot of cars at the liquor store, so John had to double-park the big Buick. "That's close enough, close enough," Mr. Lutz said. "Don't get any closer, whoa!" He was out of the car before John could bring it to a complete stop. "You and Tessie wait here," he said. "I'll go in for the liquor."

"Mr. Lutz. Say, Mr. Lutz," John called.

"Daddy!" Thelma shouted.

Mr. Lutz returned. "What is it, boys and girls?" His tone, John noticed, was becoming reedy. He was probably getting hungry.

"Here's the money they gave me." John pulled two wadded dollars from the change pocket of his dungarees. "My mother said to get something inexpensive but nice."

"Inexpensive but nice?" Mr. Lutz repeated.

"She said something about California sherry."

"What did she say about it? To get it? Or not to?"

"I guess to get it."

"You guess." Mr. Lutz shoved himself away from the car and walked backward toward the store as he talked. "You and Tessie wait in the car. Don't go off somewhere. I'll be only one minute."

John leaned back in his seat and gracefully rested one hand at the top of the steering wheel. "I like your father."

"You don't know how he acts to Mother," Thelma said.

John studied the clean line under his wrist and thumb. He flexed his wrist and watched the neat little muscles move in his forearm. "You know what I need?" he said. "A wrist-watch."

"Oh, Jan," Thelma said. "Stop admiring your own hand. It's really disgusting."

A ghost of a smile flickered over his lips, but he let his strong, nervous fingers remain as they were. "I'd sell my soul for a drag right now."

"Daddy keeps a pack in the glove compartment," Thelma said. "I'd get them if my fingernails weren't so long."

"*I'll* get it open," John said. He did. They fished one cigarette out of the old pack of Old Golds they found and took alternate puffs. "Ah," John said, "that first drag of the day, clawing and scraping its way down your throat."

"Be on the lookout for Daddy. They hate my smoking."

"Thelma."

"Yes?" She stared deep into his eyes, her face half hidden in shadow.

"Don't pluck your eyebrows."

"I think it looks nice."

"It's like calling me 'Jan.'" There was a silence, not awkward.

"Get rid of the rette, Jan. Daddy just passed the window."

Being in the liquor store had put Mr. Lutz in a soberer mood. "Here you be, John," he said, in a businesslike way. He handed John a tall, velvet-red bottle. "Better let me drive. You drive like a veteran, but I know the short cuts."

"I can walk from your house, Mr. Lutz," John said, knowing Mr. Lutz wouldn't make him walk. "Thanks an awful lot for all you've done."

"I'll drive you up. People from Philadelphia can't be kept waiting. We can't make this young man walk a mile, now can we, Tessie?" Nobody knew what to say to this last remark, so they kept quiet all the way, although several things were bothering John.

When the car stopped in front of his house, a country house but close to the road, he forced himself to ask, "Say, Mr. Lutz. I wonder if there was any change?"

"What? Oh. Goodness. I nearly forgot. You'll have your daddy thinking I'm a crook." He reached into his pocket and without looking handed John a dollar, a quarter, and a penny.

"This seems like a lot," John said. The wine must be cheap. Maybe he should have let his mother call his father at school to pick it up, like she had wanted to.

"It's your change," Mr. Lutz said.

"Well, thanks an awful lot."

"Goodbye, now, my friend," Mr. Lutz said.

"So long." John slammed the door. "Goodbye, Thelma. Don't forget what I told you." He winked.

The car pulled out, and John walked up the path. "Don't

forget what I told you," he repeated to himself, winking. The bottle was cool and heavy in his hands. He glanced at the label; it read *Château Mouton-Rothschild 1937*.

# A SENSE OF
SHELTER

SNOW FELL against the high school all day, wet big-flaked snow that did not accumulate well. Sharpening two pencils, William looked down on a parking lot that was a blackboard in reverse; car tires had cut smooth arcs of black into the white, and wherever a school bus had backed around, it had left an autocratic signature of two *V*'s. The snow, though at moments it whirled opaquely, could not quite bleach these scars away. The temperature must be exactly freezing. The window was open a crack, and a canted pane of glass lifted outdoor air into his face, coating the cedarwood scent of pencil shavings with the transparent odor of the wet window-sill. With each revolution of the handle his knuckles came within a fraction of an inch of the tilted glass, and the faint chill this proximity breathed on them sharpened William's already acute sense of shelter.

The sky behind the shreds of snow was stone-colored. The murk inside the high classroom gave the air a solidity that limited the overhead radiance to its own vessels: six globes of dull incandescence floated on the top of a thin sea. The feeling the gloom gave him was not gloomy but joyous; he felt they were all sealed in, safe; the colors of cloth were dyed deeper, the sound of whispers was made more distinct, the smells of tablet paper and wet shoes and varnish and face powder pierced him with a sharp sense of possession. These were his classmates sealed in, his, the stupid as well as the clever, the plain as well as the lovely, his enemies as well as his friends, his. He felt like a king and seemed to move to his seat between the bowed heads of subjects that loved him less than he loved them. His seat was sanctioned by tradition; for twelve years he had sat at the rear of classrooms, William Young, flanked by Marsha Wyckoff and Andy Zimmerman. Once there had been two Zimmermans, but one went to work in his father's greenhouse, and in some classes – Latin and trig – there were none, and William sat at the edge of the class as if on the lip of a cliff, and Marsha Wyckoff became Marvin Wolf or Sandra Wade. It was always a desk, though; its surface altered from hour to hour but from the blue-stained ink well his mind could extract, like a chain of magicians' handkerchiefs, memories from the first grade on.

As a senior he was a kind of king, and as a teacher's pet another kind, a puppet king, who gathered in appointive posts and even, when the vote split between two football heroes, some elective ones. He was not popular, he had never had a girl, his intense friends of childhood had drifted off into teams and gangs, and in large groups – when the whole school, for instance, went in the fall to the beautiful, dung-and-cotton-candy-smelling county fair – he was always an odd man, without a seat on the bus home. But exclusion is itself a form of inclusion. He even had a nickname: Mip, because he stuttered. Taunts no longer much frightened him; he had come late into his physical inheritance, but this summer it had arrived, and he at last stood equal with his large, boisterous parents, and had to unbutton his shirt cuffs to get his wrists through them, and discovered he could pick up a basketball with one hand. So, his long legs blocking two aisles, he felt regal even in size and, almost trembling with happiness under the high globes of light beyond whose lunar glow invisible snowflakes were drowning on the gravel roof of his castle, he could believe that the long delay of unpopularity had been merely a consolidation, that he was at last strong enough to make his move. Today he would tell Mary Landis he loved her.

He had loved her ever since, a fat-faced tomboy with freckles and green eyes, she deftly stole his rubber-lined schoolbag on the walk back from second grade along Jewett Street and outran him – simply had better legs. The superior speed a boy was supposed to have failed to come; his kidneys burned with panic. In front of the grocery store next to her home she stopped and turned. She was willing to have him catch up. This humiliation on top of the rest was too much to bear. Tears broke in his throat; he spun around and ran home and threw himself on the floor of the front parlor, where his grandfather, feet twiddling, perused the newspaper and soliloquized all morning. In time the letter slot rustled, and the doorbell rang, and Mary gave his mother the schoolbag and the two of them politely exchanged whispers. Their voices had been to him, lying there on the carpet with his head wrapped in his arms, indistinguishable. Mother had always liked Mary. From when she had been a tiny girl dancing along the hedge on the end of an older sister's arm, Mother had liked her. Out of all the children that flocked, similar as pigeons, through the neighborhood, Mother's heart had reached out as if with claws and fastened on Mary. He never took the schoolbag to school again, he refused to touch it. He supposed it was still in the attic, still faintly smelling of its rubber lining.

Fixed high on the plaster like a wren clinging to a barn wall, the buzzer sounded the two-minute signal. In the middle of the classroom Mary Landis stood up, a Monitor badge pinned to her belly. Her broad red belt was buckled with a brass bow and arrow. She wore a lavender sweater with the sleeves pushed up to expose her forearms, a delicately cheap effect. Wild stories were told about her; perhaps it was merely his knowledge of these that put the hardness in her face. Her eyes seemed braced for squinting and their green was frosted. Her freckles had faded. William thought she laughed less this year; now that she was in the Secretarial Course and he in the College Preparatory, he saw her in only one class a day, this one, English. She stood a second, eclipsed at the thighs by Jack Stephens' zebra-striped shoulders, and looked back at the class with a stiff, worn glance, as if she had seen the same faces too many times before. Her habit of perfect posture emphasized the angularity she had grown into. There was a nervous edge, a boxiness in her bones, that must have been waiting all along under the childish fat. Her eye sockets were deeply indented, and her chin had a prim set that seemed in the murky air tremulous and defiant. Her skirt was cut square and straight. Below the waist she was lean; the legs that had outrun him were still athletic; she starred at hockey and cheerleading. Above, she was ample: stacked. She turned and in switching up the aisle encountered a boy's leg thrown into her path. She coolly looked down until it withdrew. She was used to such attentions. Her pronged chest poised, Mary proceeded out the door, and someone she saw in the hall made her smile, a wide smile full of warmth and short white teeth, and love scooped at William's heart. He *would* tell her.

In another minute, the second bell rasped. Shuffling through the perfumed crowds to his next class, he crooned to himself, in the slow, over-enunciated manner of the Negro vocalist who had brought the song back this year:

> "Lah-vender blue, dilly dilly,
> Lavendih gree-heen;

84

*Eef* I were king, dilly dilly,
You would be queen."

The song gave him an exultant sliding sensation that inter-twined with the pleasures of his day. He knew all the answers, he had done all the work, the teachers called upon him only to rebuke the ignorance of the others. In trig and soc. sci. both it was this way. In gym, the fourth hour of the morning, he, who was always picked near the last, startled his side by excelling at volleyball, leaping like a madman, shouting like a bully. The ball felt light as a feather against his big bones. His hair in wet quills from the shower, he walked in the icy air to Luke's Luncheonette, where he ate three twenty-cent hamburgers in a booth with three juniors. There was Barry Kruppman, a tall, hyperthyroid-eyed boy who came on the school bus from the country town of Bows-ville and who was an amateur hypnotist; he told the tale of a Portland, Oregon, businessman who under hypnosis had been taken back through sixteen reincarnations to the condi-tion of an Egyptian concubine in the household of a high priest of Isis. There was Barry's friend Lionel Griffin, a pudgy simp whose blond hair puffed out above his ears in two slick waxed wings. He was rumored to be a fairy, and in fact did seem most excited by the transvestite aspect of the soul's transmigration. And there was Lionel's female sidekick Virginia, a drab little mystery who chain-smoked English Ovals and never said anything. She had sallow skin and smudged eyes and Lionel kept jabbing her and shrieking, making William wince. He would rather have sat with mem-bers of his own class, who filled the other booths, but he would have had to force himself on them. These juniors welcomed his company. He asked, "Wuh-well, was he ever a c-c-c-cockroach, like Archy?"

Kruppman's face grew serious; his furry lids dropped down over the bulge of his eyes, and when they drew back, his pupils were as small and hard as BBs. "That's the really interesting thing. There was this gap, see, between his being a knight under Charlemagne and then a sailor on a ship putting out from Macedonia – that's where Yugoslavia is now – in the time of Nero; there was this gap, when the only thing the guy would do was walk around the office snarling and growling, see, like this." Kruppman worked his blotched ferret face up into a snarl and Griffin shrieked. "He tried to bite one of the assistants and they think that for six hundred years" – the uncanny, unhealthy seriousness of his whisper hushed Griffin momentarily – "for six hundred years he just was a series of wolves. Probably in the German forests. You see, when he was in Macedonia" – his whisper barely audible – "he murdered a woman."

Griffin squealed in ecstasy and cried, "Oh, Kruppman! Kruppman, how you do go on!" and jabbed Virginia in the arm so hard an English Oval jumped from her hand and bobbled across the Formica table. William gazed over their heads in pain.

The crowd at the soda counter had thinned so that when the door to the outside opened he saw Mary come in and hesitate there for a second where the smoke inside and the snow outside swirled together. The mixture made a kind of – Kruppman's ridiculous story had put the phrase in his head – wolf-weather, and she was just a gray shadow caught in it alone. She bought a pack of cigarettes from Luke and went out again, a kerchief around her head, the pneumatic thing above the door hissing behind her. For a long time she had been at the center of whatever gang was the one: in the second grade the one that walked home up Jewett Street together, and in the sixth grade the one that went bicycling as far away as the quarry and the Rentschler estate and played touch football Saturday afternoons, and in the ninth grade the one that went roller-skating at Candlebridge Park with the tenth-grade boys, and in the eleventh grade the one that held parties lasting past midnight and that on Sundays drove in caravans as far as Philadelphia and back. And all the while there had been a succession of boyfriends, first Jack Stephens and Fritz March in their class and then boys a grade ahead and then Barrel Lord, who was a senior when they were sophomores and whose name was in the newspapers all football season, and then, this last summer, someone out of the school altogether, a man she met while working as a waitress in Alton. So this year her weekends were taken up, and the party gang carried on as if she had never existed, and nobody saw her much except in school and when she stopped by in Luke's to buy a pack of cigarettes. Her silhouette against the big window had looked wan, her head hooded, her face nibbled by light, her fingers fiddling on the veined counter with her coins. He yearned to reach out, to comfort her, but he was wedged deep in the shrill booths, between the jingling of the pinball machine and the twanging of the jukebox. The impulse left him with a disagreeable feeling. He had adored her too long to have his investment diminished by pity.

The two hours of the school afternoon held Latin and a study hall. In study hall, while the five people at the table with him played tic-tac-toe and sucked cough drops and yawned, he did all his homework for the next day. He prepared thirty lines of Vergil, Aeneas in the Underworld. The study hall was a huge low room in the basement of the building; its coziness crept into Tartarus. On the other side of the custard-colored wall the circular saw in the woodworking shop whined and gasped and then whined again; it bit off pieces of wood with a rising, somehow terrorized inflection – bzzzzzup! He solved ten problems in trigonometry. His mind cut neatly through their knots and separated them, neat stiff squares of answer, one by one from the long plank of problems that connected plane geometry with solid. Lastly, as the snow drifted down on a slant into the cement pits outside the steel-muntinned windows, he read a short story by Edgar Allan Poe. He closed the book softly on its pleasing final shudder. He gazed at the red, wet, menthol-scented inner membrane of Judy Whipple's yawn, rimmed with flaking pink lipstick, and yielded his conscience to the snug sense of his work done, of the snow falling, of the warm minutes that walked through their shelter so slowly. The perforated acoustic tiling above his head seemed the lining of a tube that would go all the way: high school merging into college, college into graduate school, graduate school into teaching at a college – section man, assistant, associate, *full* professor, possessor of a dozen languages and a thousand books, a man brilliant in his forties, wise in his fifties, renowned in his sixties, revered in his seventies, and then retired, serenely waiting until the time came for the last transition from silence to silence, and he would die, like Tennyson, with a copy of *Cymbeline* beside him on the moon-drenched bed.

After school he had to go to Room 101 and cut a sports cartoon into a stencil for the school paper. He liked the high school best when it was nearly empty. Then the janitors went down the halls sowing seeds of red wax and making an immaculate harvest with broad brooms, gathering all the fluff and hairpins and wrappers and powder that the animals had dropped that day. The basketball team thumped in the hollow gymnasium; the cheerleaders rehearsed behind drawn curtains on the stage. In Room 101 two empty-headed typists with stripes bleached into their hair banged away between giggles and mistakes. At her desk Mrs. Gregory, the faculty sponsor, wearily passed her pencil through misspelled news copy on tablet paper. William took the shadow box from the top of the filing cabinet and the styluses and little square plastic shading screens from their drawer and the stencil from the closet where the typed stencils hung, like fragile scarves, on hooks. "B-BALLERS BOW, 57–42," was the headline. He drew a tall b-baller bowing to a stumpy pagan idol, labelled "W" for victorious Weiserton High, and traced the drawing in the soft blue wax with the fine loop stylus. His careful breath grazed his knuckles. His eyebrows frowned while his heart bobbed happily on the giddy prattle of the typists. The shadow box was simply a black frame holding a pane of glass and lifted at one end by two legs so that the lightbulb, fitted in a metal tray, could slide underneath. As he worked, his eyes smarting, he mixed himself up with the lightbulb, felt himself burning under a slanting roof upon which a huge hand scratched. The glass grew hot; the danger in the job was pulling the softened wax with your damp hand, distorting or tearing the typed letters. Sometimes the center of an *o* stuck to your skin like a bit of blue confetti. But he was expert and cautious. He returned the things to their places feeling airily tall, heightened by Mrs. Gregory's appreciation, which she expressed by keeping her back turned, in effect stating that other staff members were undependable but William did not need to be watched.

In the hall outside Room 101 only the shouts of a basket-ball scrimmage reverberated; the chant of the cheerleaders had been silenced. Though he had done everything, he felt reluctant to leave. Neither of his parents – both worked – would be home yet, and this building was equally his home. He knew all its nooks. On the second floor of the annex, beyond the art room, there was a strange, narrow boys' lavatory that no one ever seemed to use. It was here one time that Barry Kruppman tried to hypnotize him and cure his stuttering. Kruppman's voice purred and his irises turned tiny in the bulging whites and for a moment William felt himself lean backward involuntarily, but he was distracted by the bits of bloodshot vein in the corners of those popping eyes. The folly of giving up his will to this weirdo occurred to him; he refused to let go and go under, and perhaps therefore his stuttering had continued.

The frosted window at the end of the long little room cast a watery light on the green floor and made the porcelain urinals shine like slices of moon. William washed his hands with exaggerated care, enjoying the lavish amount of powdered soap provided for him in this civic castle. He studied his face in the mirror, making infinitesimal adjustments to attain the absolutely most flattering angle, and then put his hands below his throat to get their strong, long-fingered beauty into the picture. As he walked toward the door he sang, closing his eyes and gasping as if he were a real Negro whose entire career depended upon the recording:

> "Who – told me so, dilly dilly,
>  Who told me soho?
>  *Aii* told myself, dilly dilly,
>  I told me so."

When he emerged into the hall it was not empty: one girl walked down its varnished perspective toward him, Mary Landis, a scarf on her head and books in her arms. Her locker was up here, on the second floor of the annex. His own was in the annex basement. A ticking sensation that existed neither in the medium of sound nor of light crowded against his throat. She flipped the scarf back from her hair and in a conversational voice that carried well down the clean planes of the hall said, "Hi, Billy." The name came from way back, when they were both children, and made him feel small but brave.

"Hi. How are you?"

"Fine." Her smile broadened out from the *F* of this word.

What was so funny? Was she really, as it seemed, pleased to see him? "Du-did you just get through cheer-cheer-cheer-leading?"

"Yes. Thank God. *Oh*, she's so awful. She makes us do the same stupid locomotives for every cheer; I told her, no wonder nobody cheers any more."

"This is M-M-Miss Potter?" He blushed, feeling that he made an ugly face in getting past the *M*. When he got caught in the middle of a sentence the constriction was somehow worse. He admired the way words poured up her throat, distinct and petulant.

"Yes, Potbottom Potter," she said, "she's just aching for a man and takes it out on us. I wish she would get one. Honestly, Billy, I have half a mind to quit. I'll be so glad when June comes, I'll never set foot in this idiotic building again."

Her lips, pale with the lipstick worn off, crinkled bitterly. Foreshortened from the height of his eyes, her face looked cross as a cat's. It a little shocked him that poor Miss Potter and this kind, warm school stirred her to what he had to take as actual anger; this grittiness in her was the first abrasive texture he had struck today. Couldn't she see around teachers, into their fatigue, their poverty, their fear? It had been so long since he had spoken to her, he wasn't sure how coarse she had become. "Don't quit," he brought out of his mouth at last. "It'd be n-n-n-nuh – it'd be nothing without you."

He pushed open the door at the end of the hall for her and as she passed under his arm she looked up and said, "Why, aren't you sweet?"

The stairwell, all asphalt and iron, smelled of galoshes. It felt more secret than the hall, more specially theirs; there was something magical in the rapid multiplication of planes and angles as they descended that lifted the spell on his tongue, so that words came as quickly as his feet pattered on the steps.

"No, I mean it," he said, "you're really a beautiful cheer-leader. But then you're beautiful period."

"I've skinny legs."

"Who told you that?"

"Somebody."

"Well, *he* wasn't very sweet."

"No."

"Why do you hate this poor old school?"

"Now, Billy. You know you don't care about this junky place any more than I do."

"I love it. It breaks my heart to hear you say you want to get out, because then I'll never see you again."

"You don't care, do you?"

"Why, sure I care; you *know*" – their feet stopped; they had reached bottom, the first-floor landing, two brass-barred doors and a grimy radiator – "I've always li-loved you."

"You don't mean that."

"I do too. It's ridiculous but there it is. I wanted to tell you today and now I have."

He expected her to laugh and go out the door, but instead she showed an unforeseeable willingness to discuss this awk-ward matter. He should have realized before this that women enjoy being talked to. "It's a very silly thing to say," she asserted tentatively.

"I don't see why," he said, fairly bold now that he couldn't seem more ridiculous, and yet picking his words with a certain strategic care. "It's not *that* silly to love somebody,

I mean what the hell. Probably what's silly is not to do any-thing about it for umpteen years, but, then, I never had an opportunity, I thought."

He set his books down on the radiator and she set hers down beside his. "What kind of opportunity were you wait-ing for?"

"Well, see, that's it; I didn't know." He wished, in a way, she would go out the door. But she had propped herself against the wall and plainly awaited more conversation. "Yuh-you were such a queen and I was such a nothing and I just didn't really want to presume." It wasn't very interest-ing; it puzzled him that she seemed to be interested. Her face had grown quite stern, her mouth small and thoughtful, and he made a gesture with his hands intended to release her from the bother of thinking about it. After all, it was just a disposi-tion of his heart, nothing permanent or expensive; perhaps it was just his mother's idea anyway. Half in impatience to close the account, he asked, "Will you marry me?"

"You don't want to marry me," she said. "You're going to go on and be somebody."

He blushed in pleasure; is this how she saw him, is this how they all saw him; as nothing now, but in time some-body? Had his hopes always been obvious? He dissembled, saying, "No, I'm not. But anyway, you're great now. You're so pretty, Mary."

"Oh, Billy," she said, "if you were me for just one day you'd hate it."

She said this rather blankly, watching his eyes; he wished her voice had shown more misery. In his world of closed sur-faces a panel, carelessly pushed, had opened, and he hung in this openness paralyzed, unable to think what to say. Noth-ing he could think of quite fit the abruptly immense context. The radiator cleared its throat. Its heat made, in the intimate volume just this side of the doors on whose windows the snow beat limply, a provocative snugness. He supposed he should try to kiss her, and stepped forward, his hands lifting toward her shoulders. Mary sidestepped between him and the radiator and put the scarf back on. She lifted the cloth like a broad plaid halo above her head and then wrapped it around her chin and knotted it so she looked, in her red galoshes and bulky coat, like a peasant woman in a movie about Europe. With her hair swathed, her face seemed pale and chunky, and when she recradled the books in her arms her back bent humbly. "It's too hot in here," she said. "I've got to wait for somebody." The disconnectedness of the two statements seemed natural in the fragmented atmosphere his stops and starts had produced. She bucked the brass bar with her shoulder and the door slammed open; he followed her into the weather.

"For the person who thinks your legs are too skinny?"

"Could be, Mip." As she looked up at him a snowflake caught on the lashes of one eye. She jerkily rubbed that cheek on the shoulder of her coat and stamped a foot, splashing slush. Cold water gathered on the back of his thin shirt. He put his hands in his pockets and pressed his arms against his sides to keep from shivering.

"Thuh-then you wo-won't marry me?" His instinct told him the only way back was by going forward, ridiculously.

"We don't know each other," she said.

"My God," he said. "Why not? I've known you since kindergarten."

"What do you know about me?"

This awful seriousness of hers; he must dissolve it. "That you're not a virgin." But instead of making her laugh this made her face go dead and turned it away. Like beginning to kiss her, it was a mistake. In part, he felt grateful for his

94

mistakes; they were like loyal friends who are nevertheless embarrassing. "What do you know about *me?*" he asked, setting himself up for a finishing insult but dreading it. He hated the stiff feel of his smile between his cheeks; he glimpsed, as if the snow were a mirror, how hateful he looked.

"That you're basically very nice."

Her reply blinded him to his physical discomfort, set him burning with regret. "Listen," he said, "I did love you. Let's at least get that straight."

"You never loved anybody, Billy," she said. "You don't know what it is."

"O.K.," he said. "Pardon me."

"You're excused."

"You better wait in the school," he told her. "He's-eez-eez going to be a long time."

She didn't answer and walked a little distance, along the slack cable that divided the parking lot from the softball field. One bicycle, rusted as if it had been there for years, leaned in the rack, its fenders supporting crescents of white.

The warmth inside the door felt heavy. William picked up his books and ran his pencil across the black ribs of the radiator before going down the stairs to his locker in the annex basement. The shadows were thick at the foot of the steps; suddenly it felt late, he must hurry and get home. He was seized by the irrational fear that the school authorities were going to lock him in. The cloistered odors of paper, sweat, and, from the woodshop at the far end of the basement hall, sawdust no longer flattered him; the tall green double lockers appeared to study him critically through the three air slits near their tops. When he opened his locker, and put his books on his shelf, below Marvin Wolf's, and removed his coat from his hook, his self seemed to crawl into the long dark space thus made vacant, the humiliated, ugly, educable self. In answer to a flick of his large hand the steel door weightlessly floated shut, and through the length of his body he felt so clean and free he smiled. Between now and the happy future predicted for him he had nothing, almost literally nothing, to do.

# FLIGHT

AT THE AGE OF SEVENTEEN I was poorly dressed and funny-looking, and went around thinking about myself in the third person. "Allen Dow strode down the street and home." "Allen Dow smiled a thin sardonic smile." Consciousness of a special destiny made me both arrogant and shy. Years before, when I was eleven or twelve, just on the brink of ceasing to be a little boy, my mother and I, one Sunday afternoon – my father was busy, or asleep – hiked up to the top of Shale Hill, a child's mountain that formed one side of the valley that held our town. There the town lay under us, Olinger, perhaps a thousand homes, the best and biggest of them climbing Shale Hill toward us, and beyond them the blocks of brick houses, one- and two-family, the homes of my friends, sloping down to the pale thread of the Alton Pike, which strung together the high school, the tennis courts, the movie theatre, the town's few stores and gasoline stations, the elementary school, the Lutheran church. On the other side lay more homes, including our own, a tiny white patch placed just where the land began to rise toward the opposite mountain, Cedar Top. There were rims and rims of hills beyond Cedar Top, and, looking south, we could see the pike dissolving in other towns and turning out of sight amid the patches of green and brown farmland, and it seemed the entire county was lying exposed under a thin veil of haze. I was old enough to feel uneasy at standing there alone with my mother, beside a wind-stunted spruce tree, on a long spine of shale. Suddenly she dug her fingers into the hair on my head and announced, "There we all are, and there we'll all be forever." She hesitated before the word "forever," and hesitated again before adding, "Except you, Allen. You're going to fly." A few birds were hung far out over the valley, at the level of our eyes, and in her impulsive way she had just plucked the image from them, but it felt like the clue I had been waiting all my childhood for. My most secret self had been made to respond, and I was intensely embarrassed, and irritably ducked my head out from under her melodramatic hand.

She was impulsive and romantic and inconsistent. I was never able to develop this spurt of reassurance into a steady theme between us. That she continued to treat me like an ordinary child seemed a betrayal of the vision she had made me share. I was captive to a hope she had tossed off and forgotten. My shy attempts to justify irregularities in my conduct – reading late at night or not coming back from school on time – by appealing to the image of flight were received with a startled blank look, as if I were talking nonsense. It seemed outrageously unjust. Yes, but, I wanted to say, yes, but it's *your* nonsense. And of course it was just this that made my appeal ineffective: her knowing that I had not made it mine, that I cynically intended to exploit both the privileges of being extraordinary and the pleasures of being ordinary. She feared my wish to be ordinary; once she did respond to my protest that I was learning to fly, by crying with red-faced ferocity, "You'll never learn, you'll stick and die in the dirt just like I'm doing. Why should you be better than your mother?"

She had been born ten miles to the south, on a farm she and her mother had loved. Her mother, a small fierce woman who looked more like an Arab than a German, worked in the fields with the men, and drove the wagon to market ten miles away every Friday. When still a tiny girl, my mother rode with her, and my impression of those rides is of fear – the little girl's fear of the gross and beery men who grabbed and hugged her, her fear of the wagon's breaking, of the produce's not selling, of her father's condition when at nightfall they returned. Friday was his holiday, and he drank. His drinking is impossible for me to picture, for I never knew him except as an enduring, didactic, almost Biblical old man, whose one passion was reading the newspapers and whose one hatred was of the Republican Party. There was something public about him; now that he is dead I keep seeing bits of him attached to famous politicians – his watch chain and his plump, square stomach in old films of Theodore Roosevelt, his high-top shoes and the tilt of his head in a photograph of Alfalfa Bill Murray. Alfalfa Bill is turning his head to talk, and holds his hat by the crown, pinching it between two fingers and a thumb, a gentle and courtly grip that reminded me so keenly of my grandfather that I tore the picture out of *Life* and put it in a drawer.

Laboring in the soil had never been congenial to my grandfather, though with his wife's help he prospered by it. Then, in an era when success was hard to avoid, he began to invest in stocks. In 1922 he bought our large white home in the town – its fashionable section had not yet shifted to the Shale Hill side of the valley – and settled in to reap his dividends. He believed to his death that women were foolish, and the broken hearts of his two must have seemed specially so. The dignity of finance for the indignity of farming must have struck him as an eminently advantageous exchange. It strikes me that way, too, and how to reconcile my idea of those fear-ridden wagon rides with the grief that my mother insists she and her mother felt at being taken from the farm? Perhaps prolonged fear is a ground of love. Or perhaps, and likelier, the equation is long and complex, and the few factors I know – the middle-aged woman's mannish pride of land, the adolescent girl's pleasure in riding horses across the fields, their common feeling of rejection in Olinger – are enclosed in brackets and heightened by coefficients that I cannot see. Or perhaps it is not love of land but its absence that needs explaining, in my grandfather's fastidiousness and pride. He believed that as a boy he had been overworked, and bore his father a grudge that my mother could never understand. Her grandfather to her was a saintly slender giant, over six feet tall when this was a prodigy, who knew the names of everything, like Adam in Eden. In his old age he was blind. When he came out of the house, the dogs rushed forward to lick his hands. When he lay dying, he requested a Gravenstein apple from the tree on the far edge of the meadow, and his son brought him a Krauser from the orchard near the house. The old man refused it, and my grandfather made a second trip, but in my mother's eyes the outrage had been committed, an insult without provocation. What had his father done to him? The only specific complaint I ever heard my grandfather make was that, when he was a boy and had to fetch water for the men in the fields, his father would tell him sarcastically, "Pick up your feet; they'll come down themselves." How incongruous! As if each generation of parents commits atrocities against their children which by God's decree remain invisible to the rest of the world.

I remember my grandmother as a little dark-eyed woman who talked seldom and was always trying to feed me, and then as a hook-nosed profile pink against the lemon cushions of the casket. She died when I was seven. All the rest I know about her is that she was the baby of twelve children, that while she was alive she made our yard one of the most beautiful in town, and that I am supposed to resemble her brother Pete. My mother was precocious; she was fourteen when they moved, and for three years had been attending the county normal school. She graduated from Lake College, near Philadelphia, when she was only twenty, a tall handsome girl with a self-deprecatory smile, to judge from one of the curling photographs kept in a shoebox that I was always opening as a child, as if it might contain the clue to the quarrels in my house. My mother stands at the end of our brick walk, beside the elaborately trimmed end of our privet hedge – in shape a thick square column mounted by a rough ball of leaf. The ragged arc of a lilac bush in flower cuts into the right edge of the photograph, and behind my mother I can see a vacant lot where there has been a house ever since I can remember. She poses with a kind of country grace in a long light-colored coat, unbuttoned to expose her beads and a short yet somehow demure flapper dress. Her hands are in her coat pockets, a beret sits on one side of her bangs, and there is a swank about her that seemed incongruous to me, examining this picture on the stained carpet of an ill-lit old house in the closing years of the Thirties and in the dark of the warring Forties. The costume and the girl in it look so up-to-date, so formidable. It was my grandfather's pleasure, in his prosperity, to give her a generous clothes allowance. My father, the penniless younger son of a New Jersey Presbyterian minister, had worked his way through Lake College by waiting on tables, and still speaks with mild resentment of the beautiful clothes that Lillian Baer wore. This aspect of my mother caused me some pain in high school; she was a fabric snob, and insisted on buying my slacks and sport shirts at the best store in Alton, and since we had little money, she bought me few, when of course what I needed was what my classmates had – a wide variety of cheap clothes.

At the time the photograph was taken, my mother wanted to go to New York. What she would have done there, or exactly what she wanted to do, I don't know; but her father forbade her. "Forbid" is a husk of a word today, but at that time, in that old-fashioned province, in the mouth of an "indulgent father," it apparently was still vital, for the force of that forbidding continued to be felt in the house for years, and when I was a child, as one of my mother's endless harangues to my grandfather climbed toward its weeping peak, I could feel it around and above me, like a large root encountered by an earthworm.

Perhaps in a reaction of anger my mother married my father, Victor Dow, who at least took her as far away as Wilmington, where he had made a beginning with an engineering firm. But the Depression hit, my father was laid off, and the couple came to the white brick house in Olinger, where my grandfather sat reading the newspapers that traced his stocks' decline into worthlessness. I was born. My grandmother went around as a cleaning lady, and grew things in our quarter-acre yard to sell. We kept chickens, and there was a large plot of asparagus. After she had died, in a frightened way I used to seek her in the asparagus patch. By midsummer it would be a forest of dainty green trees, some as tall as I was, and in their frothy touch a spirit seemed to speak, and in the soft thick net of their intermingling branches a promise seemed to be caught, as well as a menace. The asparagus trees were frightening; in the center of the patch, far from the house and the alley, I would fall under a spell, and become tiny, and wander among the great smooth green trunks expecting to find a little house with a smoking chimney, and in it my grandmother. She herself had believed in ghosts, which made her own ghost potent. Even now, sitting alone in my own house, I hear a board creak in the kitchen and look up fearing she will come through the doorway. And at night, just before I fall asleep, her voice calls my name in a penetrating whisper, or calls, "*Pete.*"

My mother went to work in an Alton department store, selling curtain fabric for fourteen dollars a week. During the daytime of my first year of life it was my father who took care of me. He has said since, flattering me as he always does, that it was having me on his hands that kept him from going insane. It may have been this that has made my affection for him so inarticulate, as if I were still a wordless infant looking up into the mothering blur of his male face. And that same shared year helps account, perhaps, for his gentleness with me, for his willingness to praise, as if everything I do has something sad and crippled about it. He feels sorry for me; my birth coincided with the birth of a national misery – only recently has he stopped calling me by the nickname "Young America." Around my first birthday he acquired a position teaching arithmetic and algebra in the Olinger high school, and though he was too kind and humorous to quell discipline problems, he endured his job day by day and year by year and eventually came to occupy a place in this alien town, so that I believe there are now one or two dozen ex-students, men and women nearing middle age, who carry around with them some piece of encouragement my father gave them, or remember some sentence of his that helped shape them. Certainly there are many who remember the antics with which he burlesqued his discomfort in the classroom. He kept a confiscated cap pistol in his desk, and upon getting an especially stupid answer, he would take it out and, wearing a preoccupied, regretful expression, shoot himself in the head.

My grandfather was the last to go to work. It was humbling work. He was hired by the borough crew, men who went around the streets shovelling stones and spreading tar. Bulky and ominous in their overalls, wreathed in steam, and associated with dramatic and portentous equipment, these men had grandeur in the eyes of a child, and it puzzled me, as I walked to and from elementary school, that my grandfather refused to wave to me or confess his presence in any way. Curiously strong for a fastidious man, he kept at it well into his seventies, when his sight failed. It was my task then to read his beloved newspapers to him as he sat in his chair by the bay window, twiddling his high-top shoes in the sunshine. I teased him, reading too fast, then maddeningly slow, skipping from column to column to create one long chaotic story; I read him the sports page, which did not interest him, and mumbled the editorials. Only the speed of his feet's twiddling betrayed vexation. When I'd stop, he would plead mildly in his rather beautiful, old-fashioned, elocutionary voice, "Now just the obituaries, Allen. Just the names, to see if anyone I know is there." I imagined, as I rudely barked at him the list of names that might contain the name of a friend, that I was avenging my mother; I believed that she hated him, and for her sake I tried to hate him also. From her incessant resurrection of mysterious grievances buried far back in the sunless earth of the time before I was born, I had been able to deduce only that he was an evil man, who had ruined her life, that fair creature in the beret. I did not understand. She fought with him not because she wanted to fight but because *she could not bear to leave him alone.*

Sometimes, glancing up from the sheet of print where our armies swarmed in retreat like harried insects, I would catch the old man's head in the act of lifting slightly to receive the warm sunshine on his face, a dry frail face ennobled by its thick crown of combed corn-silk hair. It would dawn on me then that his sins as a father were likely no worse than any father's. But my mother's genius was to give the people closest to her mythic immensity. I was the phoenix. My father and grandmother were legendary invader-saints, she springing out of some narrow vein of Arab blood in the German race and he crossing over from the Protestant wastes of New Jersey, both of them serving and enslaving their mates with their prodigious powers of endurance and labor. For my mother felt that she and her father alike had been destroyed by marriage, been made captive by people better yet less than they. It was true, my father had loved Mom Baer, and her death made him seem more of an alien than ever. He, and her ghost, stood to one side, in the shadows but separate from the house's dark core, the inheritance of frustration and missed opportunities that had descended from my grandfather to my mother to me, and that I, with a few beats of my grown wings, was destined to reverse and redeem.

At the age of seventeen, in the fall of my senior year, I went with three girls to debate at a high school over a hundred miles away. They were, all three, bright girls, A students; they were disfigured by A's as if by acne. Yet even so it excited me to be mounting a train with them early on a Friday morning, at an hour when our schoolmates miles away were slumping into the seats of their first class. Sunshine spread broad bars of dust down the length of the half-empty car, and through the windows Pennsylvania unfurled a brown scroll scribbled with industry. Black pipes raced beside the tracks for miles. At rhythmic intervals one of them looped upward, like the Greek letter $\Omega$. "Why does it do that?" I asked. "Is it sick?"

"Condensation?" Judith Potteiger suggested in her shy, transparent voice. She loved science.

"No," I said. "It's in pain. It's writhing! It's going to grab the train! Look out!" I ducked, honestly a little scared. All the girls laughed.

Judith and Catharine Miller were in my class, and expected me to be amusing; the third girl, a plump small junior named Molly Bingaman, had not known what to expect. It was her fresh audience I was playing to. She was the best dressed of the three, and the most poised; this made me suspect that she was the least bright. She had been substituted at the last moment for a sick member of the debating team; I knew her just by seeing her in the halls and in assembly. From a distance she seemed dumpy and prematurely adult, with a trace of a double chin. But up close she was gently fragrant, and against the weary purple cloth of the train seats her skin seemed luminous. She had beautiful skin, heartbreaking skin a pencil dot would have marred, and large blue eyes equally clear. She and I sat side by side, facing the two senior girls, who more and more took on the wan slyness of matchmakers. It was they who had made the seating arrangements.

We debated in the afternoon, and won. Yes, the German Federal Republic *should* be freed of all Allied control. The school, a posh castle on the edge of a miserable coal city, was the site of a statewide cycle of debates that was to continue into Saturday. There was a dance Friday night in the gym. I danced with Molly mostly, though to my annoyance she got in with a set of Harrisburg boys while I conscientiously pushed Judith and Catharine around the floor. We were stiff dancers, the three of us; only Molly made me seem good, floating backward from my feet fearlessly as her cheek rumpled my moist shirt. The gym was hung with orange and black crepe paper in honor of Halloween, and the pennants of all the competing schools were fastened to the walls, and a twelve-piece band pumped away blissfully on the year's sad tunes – "Heartaches," "Near You," "That's My Desire." A great cloud of balloons gathered in the steel girders was released. There was pink punch, and a local girl sang.

Judith and Catharine decided to leave before the dance was over, and I made Molly come too, though she was in a literal sweat of pleasure; her perfect skin in the oval above her neckline was flushed and glazed. I realized, with a little shock of possessiveness and pity, that she was unused to attention back home, in competition with the gorgeous Olinger ignorant.

We walked together to the house where the four of us had been boarded, a large frame house owned by an old couple and standing with lonely dignity in a semi-slum. Judith and Catharine turned up the walk, but Molly and I, with a diffident decision that I believe came from her initiative, continued, "to walk around the block." We walked miles, stopping off after midnight at a trolley-car-shaped diner. I got a hamburger, and she impressed me by ordering coffee. We walked back to the house and let ourselves in with the key we had been given; but instead of going upstairs to our rooms we sat downstairs in the dark living room and talked softly for more hours.

What did we say? I talked about myself. It is hard to hear, much less remember, what we ourselves say, just as it might be hard for a movie projector, given life, to see the shadows its eye of light is casting. A transcript, could I produce it, of my monologue through the wide turning point of that night, with all its word-by-word conceit, would distort the picture: this living room miles from home, the street light piercing the chinks in the curtains and erecting on the wallpaper rods of light the size of yardsticks, our hosts and companions asleep upstairs, the incessant sigh of my voice, coffee-primed Molly on the floor beside my chair, her stock-inged legs stretched out on the rug; and this odd sense in the room, a tasteless and odorless aura as of a pool of water widening.

I remember one exchange. I must have been describing the steep waves of fearing death that had come over me ever since early childhood, about one every three years, and I ended by supposing that it would take great courage to be an atheist. "But I bet you'll become one," Molly said. "Just to show yourself that you're brave enough." I was flattered. Within a few years, while I still remembered many of her words, I realized how touchingly gauche our assumption was that an atheist is a lonely rebel; for mobs of men are united in atheism, and oblivion – the dense leadlike sea that would occasionally sweep over me – is to them a weight as negligible as the faint pressure of their wallets in their hip pockets. This grotesque and tender misestimate of the world flares in my memory of our conversation like one of the innumerable matches we struck.

The room filled with smoke. Too weary to sit, I lay down on the floor beside her, and stroked her silver arm in silence, yet still was too timid to act on the wide and negative aura that I did not understand was of compliance. On the upstairs landing, as I went to turn into my room, Molly came forward purposefully and kissed me. With clumsy force I entered the negative space that had been waiting. Her lip-stick smeared in little unflattering flecks into the skin around her mouth; it was as if I had been given a face to eat, and the presence of bone – skull under skin, teeth behind lips – impeded me. We stood for a long time under the burning hall light, until my neck began to ache from bowing. My legs were trembling when we finally parted and sneaked into our rooms. In bed I thought, "Allen Dow tossed restlessly," and realized it was the first time that day I had thought of myself in the third person.

On Saturday morning, we lost our debate. I was sleepy and verbose and haughty, and some of the students in the audience began to boo whenever I opened my mouth. The principal came up on the stage and made a scolding speech, which finished me and my cause, untrammelled Germany. On the train back, Catharine and Judith arranged the seating so that they sat behind Molly and me, and spied on only the tops of our heads. For the first time, on that ride home, I felt what it was to bury a humiliation in the body of a woman. Nothing but the friction of my face against hers drowned out the echo of those boos. When we kissed, a red shadow would well under my lids and eclipse the hostile hooting faces of the debate audience, and when our lips parted, the bright inner sea would ebb, and there the faces would be again, more intense than ever. With a shudder of shame I'd hide my face on her shoulder, and in the warm darkness there, while a frill of her prissy collar gently scratched my nose, I felt united with Hitler and all the villains, traitors, madmen, and failures who had managed to keep, up to the moment of capture or death, a woman with them. This had puzzled me. In high school females were proud and remote; in the newspapers they were fantastic monsters of submission. And now Molly administered reassurance to me with small motions and bodily adjustments that had about them a strange flavor of the practical.

Our parents met us at the station. I was startled at how tired my mother looked. There were deep blue dents on either side of her nose, and her hair seemed somehow dissociated from her head, as if it were a ragged, half-gray wig she had put on carelessly. She had become in middle age a heavy woman, and her weight, which she usually carried upright, like a kind of wealth, had slumped away from her ownership and seemed, in the sullen light of the railway platform, to weigh on the world. I asked, "How's Grandpa?" He had taken to bed several months before, with pains in his chest.

"He still sings," she said, rather sharply. For entertainment in his increasing blindness my grandfather had long ago begun to sing, and his shapely old voice would pour forth hymns, forgotten comic ballads, and camp-meeting songs at any hour. His memory seemed to improve the longer he lived.

My mother's irritability was more manifest in the private cavity of the car; her heavy silence oppressed me. "You look so tired, Mother," I said, trying to take the offensive.

"That's nothing to how you look," she answered. "What happened up there? You stoop like an old married man."

"Nothing happened," I lied. My cheeks were parched, as if her high steady anger had the power of giving sunburn.

"I remember that Bingaman girl's mother when we first moved to town. She was the smuggest little snip north of the pike. They're real old Olinger stock, you know. They have no use for hillbillies."

My father tried to change the subject. "Well, you won one debate, Allen, and that's more than I would have done. I don't see how you do it."

"Why, he gets it from you, Victor. I've never won a debate with you."

"He gets it from Pop Baer. If that man had gone into politics, Lillian, all the misery of his life would have been avoided."

"Dad was never a debater. He was a bully. Don't go with little women, Allen. It puts you too close to the ground."

"I'm not *going* with *any*body, Mother. Really, you're so fanciful."

"Why, when she stepped off the train, from the way her chins bounced I thought she had eaten a canary. And then making my poor son, all skin and bones, carry her bag. When she walked by me I honestly was afraid she'd spit in my eye."

"I had to carry somebody's bag. I'm sure she doesn't know who you are." Though it was true I had talked a good deal about my family the night before.

My mother turned away from me. "You see, Victor – he defends her. When I was his age that girl's mother gave me a cut I'm still bleeding from, and my own son attacks me on behalf of her fat little daughter. I wonder if her mother put her up to catching him."

"Molly's a nice girl," my father interceded. "She never gave me any trouble in class, like some of those smug bastards." But he was curiously listless, for so Christian a man, in pronouncing this endorsement.

I discovered that nobody wanted me to go with Molly Bingaman. My friends – for on the strength of being funny I did have some friends, classmates whose love affairs went on over my head but whom I could accompany, as clown, on communal outings – never talked with me about Molly, and when I brought her to their parties gave the impression of ignoring her, so that I stopped taking her. Teachers at school would smile an odd tight smile when they saw us leaning by her locker or hanging around in the stairways. The eleventh-grade English instructor – one of my "boosters" on the faculty, a man who was always trying to "challenge" me, to "exploit" my "potential" – took me aside and told me how dense she was. She just couldn't grasp the logical principles of restrictive and non-restrictive clauses. He confided her parsing mistakes to me as if they betrayed – as indeed in a way they did – limits that her graceful social manner concealed. Even the Fabers, an ultra-Republican couple who ran a luncheonette near the high school, showed pleasure whenever Molly and I broke up, and persistently treated my attachment as being a witty piece of play, like my pretense with Mr. Faber of being a Communist. The entire town seemed ensnarled in my mother's myth, that escape was my proper fate. It was as if I were a sport that the ghostly elders of Olinger had segregated from the rest of the livestock and agreed to donate in time to the air; this fitted with the ambiguous sensation I had always had in the town, of being simultaneously flattered and rejected.

Molly's parents disapproved because in their eyes my family was déclassé. It was so persistently hammered into me that I was too good for Molly that I scarcely considered the proposition that, by another scale, she was too good for me. Further, Molly herself shielded me. Only once, exasperated by some tedious, condescending confession of mine, did she state that her mother didn't like me. "Why not?" I asked, genuinely surprised. I admired Mrs. Bingaman – she was beautifully preserved – and I always felt jolly in her house, with its white woodwork and matching furniture and vases of iris posing before polished mirrors.

"Oh, I don't know. She thinks you're flippant."

"But that's not true. Nobody takes himself more seriously than I do."

While Molly protected me from the Bingaman side of the ugliness, I conveyed the Dow side more or less directly to her. It infuriated me that nobody allowed me to be proud of her. I kept, in effect, asking her, Why was she stupid in English? Why didn't she get along with my friends? Why did she look so dumpy and smug? – this last despite the fact that she often, especially in intimate moments, looked beautiful to me. I was especially angry with her because this affair had brought out an ignoble, hysterical, brutal aspect of my mother that I might never have had to see otherwise. I had hoped to keep things secret from her, but even if her intuition had not been relentless, my father, at school, knew everything. Sometimes, indeed, my mother said that she didn't care if I went with Molly; it was my father who was upset. Like a frantic dog tied by one leg, she snapped in any direction, mouthing ridiculous fancies – such as that Mrs. Bingaman had pushed Molly on me just to keep me from going to college and giving the Dows something to be proud of – that would make us both suddenly start laughing. Laughter in that house that winter had a guilty sound. My grandfather was dying, and lay upstairs singing and coughing and weeping as the mood came to him, and we were too poor to hire a nurse, and too kind and cowardly to send him to a "home." It was still his house, after all. Any noise he made seemed to slash my mother's heart, and she was unable to sleep upstairs near him, and waited the nights out on the sofa downstairs. In her desperate state she would say unforgivable things to me even while the tears streamed down her face. I've never seen so many tears as I saw that winter.

Every time I saw my mother cry, it seemed I had to make Molly cry. I developed a skill at it; it came naturally to an only child who had been surrounded all his life by unhappy adults. Even in the heart of intimacy, half naked each of us, I would say something to keep her at a distance. We never made love in the final, coital sense. My reason was a mixture of idealism and superstition; I felt that if I took her virginity she would be mine forever. I depended overmuch on a technicality; she gave herself to me anyway, and I took her anyway, and have her still, for the longer I travel in a direction I could not have travelled with her the more clearly she seems the one person who loved me without advantage. I was a homely, comically ambitious poor boy, and I even refused to tell her I loved her, to pronounce the word "love" – an icy piece of pedantry that shocks me now that I have almost forgotten the pressured context in which it seemed wise.

In addition to my grandfather's illness, and my mother's grief, and my waiting to hear if I had won a scholarship to the one college that seemed good enough for me, I was burdened with managing too many petty affairs of my graduating class. I was in charge of yearbook write-ups, art editor of the school paper, chairman of the Class Gift Committee, director of the Senior Assembly, and teachers' workhorse. Frightened by my father's tales of nervous breakdowns he had seen, I kept listening for the sounds of my brain snapping, and the image of that gray, infinitely interconnected mass seemed to extend outward, to become my whole world, one dense organic dungeon, and I felt I had to get out; if I could just get out of this, into June, it would be blue sky, and I would be all right for life.

One Friday night in spring, after trying for over an hour to write thirty-five affectionate words for the yearbook about a null girl in the Secretarial Course I had never spoken a word to, I heard my grandfather begin coughing upstairs with a sound like dry membrane tearing, and I panicked. I called up the stairs, "Mother! I must go out."

"It's nine o'clock."

"I know, but I have to. I'm going crazy."

Without waiting to hear her answer or to find a coat, I left the house and backed our old car out of the garage. The weekend before, I had broken up with Molly again. All week I hadn't spoken to her, though I had seen her once in Faber's, with a boy in her class, averting her face while I, hanging by the side of the pinball machine, made rude wisecracks in her direction. I didn't dare go up to her door and knock so late at night; I just parked across the street and watched the lit windows of her house. Through their living-room window I could see one of Mrs. Bingaman's vases of hothouse iris standing on a white mantel, and my open car window admitted the spring air, which delicately smelled of wet ashes. Molly was probably out on a date with that moron in her class. But then the Bingamans' door opened, and her figure appeared in the rectangle of light. Her back was toward me, a coat was on her arm, and her mother seemed to be shouting. Molly closed the door and ran down off the porch and across the street and quickly got into the car, her eyes downcast. *She came.* When I have finally forgotten everything else – her powdery fragrance, her lucid cool skin, the way her lower lip was like a curved pillow of two cloths, the dusty red outer and wet pink inner – I'll still be grieved by this about Molly, that she came to me.

After I returned her to her house – she told me not to worry, her mother enjoyed shouting – I went to the all-night diner just beyond the Olinger town line and ate three hamburgers, ordering them one at a time, and drank two glasses of milk. It was after one o'clock when I got home, but my mother was still awake. She lay on the sofa in the dark, with the radio sitting on the floor murmuring Dixieland piped up from New Orleans by way of Philadelphia. Radio music was a steady feature of her insomniac life; not only did it help drown out the noise of her father upstairs but she seemed to enjoy it in itself. She would resist my father's pleas to come to bed by saying that the New Orleans program was not over yet. The radio was an old Philco we had always had; I had once drawn a fish on the orange disc of its celluloid dial, which had looked to my eyes like a fishbowl.

Her loneliness caught at me; I went into the living room

and sat on a chair with my back to the window. For a long time she looked at me tensely out of the darkness. "Well," she said at last, "how was little hotpants?" The vulgarity this affair had brought out in her language appalled me.

"I made her cry," I told her.

"Why do you torment the girl?"

"To please you."

"It doesn't please me."

"Well, then, stop nagging me."

"I'll stop nagging you if you'll solemnly tell me you're willing to marry her."

I said nothing to this, and after waiting she went on in a different voice, "Isn't it funny, that you should show this weakness?"

"Weakness is a funny way to put it when it's the only thing that gives me strength."

"Does it really, Allen? Well. It may be. I forget, you were born here."

Upstairs, close to our heads, my grandfather, in a voice frail but still melodious, began to sing: "There is a happy land, far, far away, where saints in glory stand, bright, bright as day." We listened, and his voice broke into coughing, a terrible rending cough growing in fury, struggling to escape, and loud with fear he called my mother's name. She didn't stir. His voice grew enormous, a bully's voice, as he repeated, "Lillian! Lillian!" and I saw my mother's shape quiver with the force coming down the stairs into her; she was like a dam; and then the power, as my grandfather fell momentarily silent, flowed toward me in the darkness, and I felt intensely angry, and hated that black mass of suffering, even while I realized, with a rapid, light calculation, that I was too weak to withstand it.

In a dry tone of certainty and dislike – how hard my heart

had become! – I told her, "All right. You'll win this one, Mother; but it'll be the last one you'll win."

My pang of fright, following this unprecedentedly cold insolence, blotted my senses; the chair ceased to be felt under me, and the walls and furniture of the room fell away – there was only the dim orange glow of the radio dial down below. In a husky voice that seemed to come across a great distance my mother said, with typical melodrama, "Goodbye, Allen."

# THE HAPPIEST
# I'VE BEEN

NEIL HOVEY came for me wearing a good suit. He parked his father's gray Chrysler on the dirt ramp by our barn and got out and stood by the open car door in a double-breasted tan gabardine suit, his hands in his pockets and his hair combed with water, squinting up at a lightning rod an old hurricane had knocked crooked.

We were driving to Chicago, so I had dressed in worn-out slacks and an outgrown corduroy shirt. But Neil was the friend I had always been most relaxed with, so I wasn't very disturbed. My parents and I walked out from the house, across the low stretch of lawn that was mostly mud after the thaw that had come on Christmas Day, and my grandmother, though I had kissed her goodbye inside the house, came out onto the porch, stooped and rather angry-looking, her head haloed by wild old woman's white hair and the hand more severely afflicted by Parkinson's disease waggling at her breast in a worried way. It was growing dark and my grandfather had gone to bed. "Nev-er trust the man who wears the red necktie and parts his hair in the middle," had been his final advice to me.

We had expected Neil since midafternoon. Nineteen, almost twenty, I was a college sophomore home on vacation; that fall I had met in a fine-arts course a girl I had fallen in love with, and she had invited me to the New Year's party her parents always gave and to stay at her house a few nights. She lived in Chicago and so did Neil now, though he had gone to our high school. His father did something – sell steel was my impression, a huge man opening a briefcase and saying, "The I-beams are very good this year" – that required him to be always on the move, so that at about thirteen Neil had been boarded with Mrs. Hovey's parents, the Lancasters. They had lived in Olinger since the town was incorporated. Indeed, old Jesse Lancaster, whose sick larynx whistled when he breathed to us boys his shocking and uproarious thoughts on the girls that walked past his porch all day long, had twice been burgess. Neil's father meanwhile got a stationary job, but he let Neil stay to graduate; after the night he graduated, Neil drove throughout the next day to join his parents. From Chicago to this part of Pennsylvania was seventeen hours. In the twenty months he had been gone Neil had come east fairly often; he loved driving and Olinger was the one thing he had that was close to a childhood home. In Chicago he was working in a garage and getting his overlapping teeth straightened by the Army so they could draft him. Korea was on. He had to go back, and I wanted to go, so it was a happy arrangement. "You're all dressed up," I accused him immediately.

"I've been saying goodbye." The knot of his necktie was loose and the corners of his mouth were rubbed with pink. Years later my mother recalled how that evening his breath to her stank so strongly of beer she was frightened to let me go with him. "*Your* grandfather always thought *his* grandfather was a very dubious character," she said then.

My father and Neil put my suitcases into the trunk; they contained all the clothes I had brought home, for the girl and I were going to go back to college on the train together, and I would not see my home again until spring.

"Well, goodbye, boys," my mother said. "I think you're both very brave." In regard to me she meant the girl as much as the roads.

"Don't you worry, Mrs. Nordholm," Neil told her quickly. "He'll be safer than in his bed. I bet he sleeps from here to Indiana." He looked at me with an irritating imitation of her own fond gaze. When they shook hands goodbye it was with an equality established on the base of my helplessness. His being so slick startled me, but, then, you can have a friend for years and never see how he operates with adults.

I embraced my mother and over her shoulder tried to take, with the camera of my head, a snapshot I could keep of the house, the woods behind it and the sunset behind them, the bench beneath the walnut tree where my grandfather cut apples into skinless bits and fed them to himself, and the ruts in the soft lawn the bakery truck had made that morning.

We started down the half-mile of dirt road to the highway that, one way, went through Olinger to the city of Alton and, the other way, led through farmland to the Turnpike. It was luxurious after the stress of farewell to two-finger a cigarette out of the pack in my shirt pocket. My family knew I smoked but I didn't do it in front of them; we were all too sensitive to bear the awkwardness. I lit mine and held the match for Neil. It was a relaxed friendship. We were about the same height and had the same degree of athletic incompetence and the same curious lack of whatever it was that aroused loyalty and compliance in beautiful girls. But it seemed to me the most important thing – about both our friendship and our failures to become, for all the love we felt for women, actual lovers – was that he and I lived with grandparents. This improved both our backward and forward vistas; we knew about the bedside commodes and midnight coughing fits that awaited most men, and we had a sense of childhoods before 1900, when the farmer ruled the land and America faced west. We had gained a dimension that made us gentle and humorous among peers but diffident at dances and hesitant in cars. Girls hate boys' doubts: they amount to insults. Gentleness is for married women to appreciate. (This is my thinking then.) A girl who has received out of nowhere a gift worth all Africa's ivory and Asia's gold wants more than just a good guy to bestow it on.

Coming onto the highway, Neil turned right toward Olinger instead of left toward the Turnpike. My reaction was to twist and assure myself through the rear window that, though a pink triangle of sandstone stared through the bare treetops, nobody at my house could possibly see.

When he was again in third gear, Neil asked, "Are you in a hurry?"

"No. Not especially."

"Schuman's having his New Year's party two days early so we can go. I thought we'd go for a couple hours and miss the Friday-night stuff on the Pike." His mouth moved and closed carefully over the dull, silver, painful braces.

"Sure," I said. "I don't care." In everything that followed there was this sensation of my being picked up and carried.

It was four miles from the farm to Olinger; we entered by Buchanan Road, driving past the tall white brick house I had lived in until I was thirteen. My grandfather had bought it before I was born and his stocks became bad, which had happened in the same year. The new owners had strung colored bulbs all along the front-door frame and the edges of the porch roof. Downtown the cardboard Santa Claus still nodded in the drugstore window but the loudspeaker on the undertaker's lawn had stopped broadcasting carols. It was quite dark now, so the arches of red and green lights above Grand Avenue seemed miracles of lift; in daylight you saw the bulbs were just hung from a straight cable by cords of different lengths. Larry Schuman lived on the other side of

126

town, the newer side. Lights ran all the way up the front edges of his house and across the rain gutter. The next-door neighbor had a plywood reindeer-and-sleigh floodlit on his front lawn and a snowman of papier-mâché leaning tipsily (his eyes were $x$'s) against the corner of his house. No real snow had fallen yet that winter. The air this evening, though, hinted that harder weather was coming.

The Schumans' living room felt warm. In one corner a blue spruce drenched with tinsel reached to the ceiling; around its pot surged a drift of wrapping paper and ribbon and boxes, a few still containing presents, gloves and diaries and other small properties that hadn't yet been absorbed into the mainstream of affluence. The ornamental balls were big as baseballs and all either crimson or indigo; the tree was so well dressed I felt self-conscious in the same room with it, without a coat or tie and wearing an old green shirt too short in the sleeves. Everyone else was dressed for a party. Then Mr. Schuman stamped in comfortingly, crushing us all into one underneath his welcome, Neil and me and the three other boys who had showed up so far. He was dressed to go out on the town, in a camel topcoat and silvery silk muffler, smoking a cigar with the band still on. You could see in Mr. Schuman where Larry got the red hair and white eyelashes and the self-confidence, but what in the son was smirking and pushy was in the father shrewd and masterful. What the one used to make you nervous the other used to put you at ease. While Mr. was jollying us, Zoe Loessner, a new interest of Larry's and the only other girl at the party so far, was talking nicely to Mrs., nodding with her entire neck and fingering her Kresge pearls and blowing cigarette smoke through a corner of her mouth, to keep it away from the middle-aged woman's face. Each time Zoe spat out a plume, the shelf of honey hair overhanging her temple bobbed. Mrs. Schuman beamed serenely above her mink coat and rhinestone pocketbook. It was odd to see her dressed in the trappings of the prosperity that usually supported her good nature invisibly, like a firm mattress under a bright homely quilt. Everybody loved her. She was a prime product of the county, a Pennsylvania Dutch woman with sons, who loved feeding her sons and who imagined that the entire world, like her life, was going well. I never saw her not smile, except at her husband. At last she moved him into the outdoors. He turned at the threshold and did a trick with his knees and called in to us, "Be good, and if you can't be good, be careful."

With them out of the way, the next item was getting liquor. It was a familiar business. Did anybody have a forged driver's license? If not, who would dare to forge theirs? Larry could provide India ink. Then again, Larry's older brother Dale might be home and would go if it didn't take too much time. However, on weekends he often went straight from work to his fiancée's apartment and stayed until Sunday. If worse came to worst, Larry knew an illegal place in Alton, but they really soaked you. The problem was solved strangely. More people were arriving all the time and one of them, Cookie Behn, who had been held back one year and hence was deposited in our grade, announced that last November he had become in honest fact twenty-one. I at least gave Cookie my share of the money feeling a little queasy, sin had become so handy.

The party was the party I had been going to all my life, beginning with Ann Mahlon's first Halloween party, which I attended as a hot, lumbering, breathless, and blind Donald Duck. My mother had made the costume, and the eyes kept slipping, and were farther apart than my eyes, so that even when the clouds of gauze parted it was to reveal the frustrating depthless world seen with one eye. Ann, who because her mother loved her so much as a child had remained somewhat childish, and I and another boy and girl who were not involved in any romantic crisis went down into the Schumans' basement to play circular Ping-Pong. Armed with paddles, we stood each at a side of the table and when the ball was stroked ran around it counterclockwise, slapping the ball and screaming. To run better, the girls took off their heels and ruined their stockings on the cement floor. Their faces and arms and shoulder sections became flushed, and when a girl lunged forward toward the net the stiff neckline of her semi-formal dress dropped away and the white arcs of her brassiere could be glimpsed cupping fat, and when she reached high her shaved armpit gleamed like a bit of chicken skin. An earring of Ann's flew off and the two connected rhinestones skidded to lie near the wall, among the Schumans' power mower and badminton poles and empty bronze motor-oil cans twice punctured by triangles. All these images were immediately lost in the whirl of our running; we were dizzy before we stopped. Ann leaned on me getting back into her shoes.

When we pushed it open the door leading down into the cellar banged against the newel post of the carpeted stairs going to the second floor; a third of the way up these, a couple sat discussing. The girl, Jacky Iselin, cried without emotion – the tears and nothing else, like water flowing over wood. Some people were in the kitchen mixing drinks and making noise. In the living room others danced to records: 78s then, stiff discs stacked in a ponderous leaning cylinder on the spindle of the Schumans' console. Every three minutes with a click and a crash another dropped and the mood abruptly changed. One moment it would be "Stay as Sweet as You Are": Clarence Lang with the absolute expression of an idiot standing and rocking monotonously with June Kaufmann's boneless sad brown hand trapped in his and their faces, staring in the same direction, pasted together like the facets of an idol. The music stopped; when they parted, a big squarish dark patch stained the cheek of each. Then, the next moment, it would be Goodman's "Loch Lomond" or "Cherokee," and nobody but Margaret Lento wanted to jitterbug. She was a former interest of Larry's who was attending the party anyway; she lived outside of Olinger and had come with another girl. Mad, she danced by herself, swinging her head recklessly and snapping her backside; a corner of her skirt flipped a Christmas ball onto the rug, where it shattered into a dozen convex reflectors. Female shoes were scattered in pairs about the room. Some were flats, resting under the sofa shyly toed in; others were high heels lying cockeyed, the spike of one thrust into its mate.

Sitting alone and ignored in a great armchair, I experienced within a warm keen dishevelment, as if there were real tears in my eyes. Had things been less unchanged they would have seemed less tragic. But the girls who had stepped out of these shoes were with few exceptions the ones who had attended my life's party. The alterations were so small: a haircut, an engagement ring, a franker plumpness. While they wheeled above me I sometimes caught from their faces an unfamiliar glint, off of a hardness I did not remember, as if beneath their skins these girls were growing more dense. The brutality added to the features of the boys I knew seemed a more willed effect, more desired and so less grievous. Considering that there was a war on, surprisingly many were present, 4-F or at college or simply waiting to be called. Shortly before midnight the door rattled and there, under the porchlight, looking forlorn and chilled in their brief athletic jackets, stood three members of the class ahead of ours who in the old days always tried to crash Schuman's parties. At Olinger High they had been sports stars, and they still stood with that well-coördinated looseness, a look of dangling from strings. The three of them had enrolled together at Melanchthon, a small Lutheran college on the edge of Alton, and in this season played on the Melanchthon basketball team. That is, two did; the third hadn't been good enough. Schuman, out of cowardice more than mercy, let them in, and they hid without hesitation in the basement, and didn't bother us, having brought their own bottle.

There was one novel awkwardness. Darryl Bechtel had married Emmy Johnson and the couple came. Darryl had worked in his father's greenhouse and was considered dull; it was Emmy that we knew. At first no one danced with her, and Darryl didn't know how, but then Schuman, perhaps as host, dared. Others followed, but Schuman had her in his arms most often, and at midnight, when we were pretending the new year began, he kissed her; a wave of kissing swept the room now, and everyone struggled to kiss Emmy. Even I did. There was something about her being married that made it extraordinary. Her cheeks in flame, she kept glancing around for rescue, but Darryl, embarrassed to see his wife dance, had gone into old man Schuman's den, where Neil sat brooding, sunk in mysterious sorrow.

When the kissing subsided and Darryl emerged, I went in to see Neil. He was holding his face in his hands and tapping his foot to a record playing on Mr. Schuman's private phonograph: Krupa's "Dark Eyes." The arrangement was droning and circular and Neil had kept the record going for hours. He loved saxophones; I guess all of us children of that Depression vintage did. I asked him, "Do you think the traffic on the Turnpike has died down by now?"

He lifted down the tall glass on the cabinet beside him and

took a convincing swallow. His face from the side seemed lean and somewhat blue. "Maybe," he said, staring at the ice cubes submerged in the ochre liquid. "The girl in Chicago's expecting you?"

"Well, yeah, but we can call and let her know, once *we* know."

"You think she'll spoil?"

"How do you mean?"

"I mean, won't you be seeing her all the time after we get there? Aren't you going to marry her?"

"I have no idea. I might."

"Well, then: you'll have the rest of Kingdom Come to see her." He looked directly at me, and it was plain in the blur of his eyes that he was sick-drunk. "The trouble with you guys that have all the luck," he said slowly, "is that you don't give a fuck about us that don't have any." Such an assault coming from Neil surprised me, as had his blarney with my mother hours before. In trying to evade his wounded stare, I discovered there was another person in the room: a girl sitting with her shoes on, reading *Holiday*. Though she held the magazine in front of her face I knew from her clothes and her unfamiliar legs that she was the friend Margaret Lento had brought. Margaret didn't come from Olinger but from Riverside, a section of Alton, not a suburb. She had met Larry Schuman at a summer job in a restaurant and for the rest of high school they had more or less gone together. Since then, though, it had dawned on Mr. and Mrs. Schuman that even in a democracy class distinctions exist, probably welcome news to Larry. In the cruellest and most stretched-out way he could manage he had been breaking off with her throughout the year now nearly ended. I had been surprised to find her at this party. Obviously she had felt shaky about attending and had brought the friend as the only kind of protection she could afford. The other girl was acting just like a guard hired for the night.

There being no answer to Neil, I went into the living room, where Margaret, insanely drunk, was throwing herself around as if wanting to break a bone. Somewhat in time to the music she would run a few steps, then snap her body like a whip, her chin striking her chest and her hands flying backward, fingers fanned, as her shoulders pitched forward. In her state, her body was childishly plastic; unharmed, she would bounce back from this jolt and begin to clap and kick and hum. Schuman stayed away from her. Margaret was small, not more than 5'2", with the smallness ripeness comes to early. She had bleached a section of her black hair platinum, cropped her head all over, and trained the stubble into short curls like those on antique statues of boys. Her face seemed quite coarse from the front, so her profile was classical unexpectedly. She might have been Portia. When she was not putting on her savage pointless dance she was in the bathroom being sick. The pity and the vulgarity of her exhibition made everyone who was sober uncomfortable; our common guilt in witnessing this girl's rites brought us so close together in that room that it seemed never, not in all time, could we be parted. I myself was perfectly sober. I had the impression then that people only drank to stop being unhappy, and I nearly always felt at least fairly happy.

Luckily, Margaret was in a sick phase around one o'clock, when the elder Schumans came home. They looked in at us briefly. It was a pleasant joke to see in their smiles that, however corrupt and unwinking we felt, to them we looked young and sleepy: Larry's friends. Things quieted after they went up the stairs. In half an hour people began coming out of the kitchen balancing cups of coffee. By two o'clock four girls stood in aprons at Mrs. Schuman's sink, and others

133

were padding back and forth carrying glasses and ashtrays. Another blameless racket pierced the clatter in the kitchen. Out on the cold grass the three Melanchthon athletes had set up the badminton net and in the faint glow given off by the house were playing. The bird, ascending and descending through uneven bars of light, glimmered like a firefly.

Now that the party was dying, Neil's apathy seemed deliberately exasperating, even vindictive. For at least another hour he persisted in hearing "Dark Eyes" over and over again, holding his head and tapping his foot. The entire scene in the den had developed a fixity that was uncanny; the girl remained in the chair and read magazines, *Holiday* and *Esquire*, one after another. In the meantime, cars came and went and raced their motors out front. Larry Schuman had taken Ann Mahlon off and didn't come back; that left Zoe Loessner to be driven home by Mr. and Mrs. Bechtel. The athletes had carried the neighbor's artificial snowman into the center of the street and disappeared. Somehow in the shuffle of arrangements at the end Neil had contracted to drive Margaret and the other girl home. Margaret was convalescing in the downstairs bathroom. I unlocked a little glass bookcase ornamenting a desk in the dark dining room and removed a volume of Thackeray's Works. It turned out to be Volume II of *Henry Esmond*. I began it, rather than break another book out of the set, which had been squeezed in there so long the bindings had sort of interpenetrated.

Henry was going off to war again when Neil finally appeared in the archway and said, "O.K., Norseman. Let's go to Chicago." "Norseman" was a variant of my name he used only when feeling special affection.

We turned off all the lamps and left the hall bulb burning against Larry's return. Margaret Lento seemed chastened. Neil gave her his arm and led her into the back seat of his father's stately car; I stood aside to let the other girl get in with her, but Neil indicated that I should sit in the back. I supposed he realized this left only the mute den-girl to go up front with him. She sat well over on her side, was all I noticed. Neil backed into the street and with unusual care steered past the snowman. Our headlights made vivid the fact that the snowman's back was a hollow right-angled gash; he had been built up against the corner of a house.

From Olinger, Riverside was diagonally across Alton. The city was sleeping as we drove through it. Most of the stop-lights were blinking green. Among cities Alton had a bad reputation; its graft and gambling and easy juries and bawdy houses were supposedly notorious throughout the Middle Atlantic states. But to me it always presented an innocent face: row after row of houses built of a local dusty-red brick the shade of flowerpots, each house fortified with a tiny, awn-inged, balustraded porch, and nothing but the wealth of movie houses and beer signs along its main street to suggest that its citizens loved pleasure more than the run of man-kind. Indeed, as we moved at moderate speed down these hushed streets bordered with parked cars, a limestone church bulking at every corner and the sodium streetlamps keeping watch from above, Alton seemed less the ultimate center of an urban region than itself a suburb of some vast mythical metropolis, like Pandemonium or Paradise. I was conscious of evergreen wreaths on door after door and of stained-glass fanlights in which each house number was embedded. I was also conscious that every block was one block farther from the Turnpike.

Riverside, fitted into the bends of the Schuylkill, was not so regularly laid out. Margaret's house was one of a short row, composition-shingled, which we approached from the rear, down a short cement alley speckled with drains. The porches were a few inches higher than the alley. Margaret asked us if we wanted to come in for a cup of coffee, since we were going to Chicago; Neil accepted by getting out of the car and slamming his door. The noise filled the alley, alarming me. I wondered at the easy social life that evidently existed among my friends at three-thirty in the morning. Margaret did, however, lead us in stealthily, and she turned on only the kitchen switch. The kitchen was divided from the living room by a large sofa, which faced into a littered gloom wherein distant light from beyond the alley spilled over the windowsill and across the spines of a radiator. In one corner the glass of a television set showed; the screen would seem absurdly small now, but then it seemed disproportionately elegant. The shabbiness everywhere would not have struck me so definitely if I hadn't just come from Schuman's place. Neil and the other girl sat on the sofa; Margaret held a match to a gas burner and, as the blue flame licked an old kettle, doled instant coffee into four flowered cups.

Some man who had once lived in this house had built by the kitchen's one window a breakfast nook, nothing more than a booth, a table between two high-backed benches. I sat in it and read all the words I could see: "Salt," "Pepper," "Have Some Lumps," "December," "Mohn's Milk Inc. – A Very Merry Christmas and Joyous New Year – Mohn's Milk Is *Safe* Milk – 'Mommy, Make It Mohn's!,'" "matches," "*HOTPOINT*," "press," "Magee Stove Federal & Furnace Corp.," "God Is In This House," "Ave Maria Gratia Plena," "Shredded Wheat Benefits Exciting New Pattern Kungsholm." After serving the two on the sofa, Margaret came to me with coffee and sat down opposite me in the booth. Fatigue had raised two blue welts beneath her eyes.

"Well," I asked her, "did you have a good time?"

She smiled and glanced down and made the small sound "Ch," vestigial of "Jesus." With absent-minded delicacy she stirred her coffee, lifting and replacing the spoon without a ripple.

"Rather odd at the end," I said, "not even the host there."

"He took Ann Mahlon home."

"I know." I was surprised that she knew, having been sick in the bathroom for that hour.

"You sound jealous," she added.

"Who does? I do? I don't."

"You like her, John, don't you?" Her using my first name and the quality of her question did not, although except for a few parties we had hardly met, seem forward, considering the hour and that she had brought me coffee. There is very little further to go with a girl who has brought you coffee.

"Oh, I like everybody," I told her, "and the longer I've known them the more I like them, because the more they're me. The only people I like better are ones I've just met. Now, Ann Mahlon I've known since kindergarten. Every day her mother used to bring her to the edge of the schoolyard for months after all the other mothers had stopped." I wanted to cut a figure in Margaret's eyes, but they were too dark. Stoically she had gotten on top of her weariness, but it was growing bigger under her.

"Did you like her then?"

"I felt sorry for her being embarrassed by her mother."

She asked me, "What was Larry like when he was little?"

"Oh, bright. Kind of mean."

"Was he mean?"

"I'd say so. Yes. In some grade or other he and I began to play chess together. I always won until secretly he took

137

lessons from a man his parents knew and read strategy books."

Margaret laughed, genuinely pleased. "Then did he win?"

"Once. After that I really tried, and after *that* he decided chess was kid stuff. Besides, I was used up. He'd have these runs on people where you'd be down at his house every afternoon, then in a couple months he'd get a new pet and that'd be that."

"He's funny," she said. "He has a kind of cold mind. He decides on what he wants, then he does what he has to do, you know, and nothing anybody says can change him."

"He does tend to get what he wants," I admitted guardedly, realizing that to her this meant her. Poor bruised little girl, in her mind he was all the time cleaving with rare cunning through his parents' objections straight to her.

My coffee was nearly gone, so I glanced toward the sofa in the other room. Neil and the girl had sunk out of sight behind its back. Before this it had honestly not occurred to me that they had a relationship, but now that I saw, it seemed plausible and, at this time of night, good news, though it meant we would not be going to Chicago yet.

So I talked to Margaret about Larry, and she responded, showing really quite an acute sense of him. To me, considering so seriously the personality of a childhood friend, as if overnight he had become a factor in the world, seemed absurd; I couldn't deeply believe that even in her world he mattered much. Larry Schuman, in little more than a year, had become nothing to me. The important thing, rather than the subject, was the conversation itself – the quick agreements, the slow nods, the weave of different memories; it was like one of those Panama baskets shaped underwater around a worthless stone.

She offered me more coffee. When she returned with it,

she sat down, not opposite, but beside me, lifting me to such a pitch of gratitude and affection the only way I could think to express it was by *not* kissing her, as if a kiss were another piece of abuse women suffered. She said, "Cold. Cheap bastard turns the thermostat down to sixty," meaning her father. She drew my arm around her shoulders and folded my hand around her bare forearm, to warm it. The back of my thumb fitted against the curve of one breast. Her head went into the hollow where my arm and chest joined; she was terribly small, measured against your own body. Perhaps she weighed a hundred pounds. Her lids lowered and I kissed her two lush eyebrows and then the spaces of skin between the rough curls, some black and some bleached, that fringed her forehead. Other than this I tried to keep as still as a bed would be. It *had* grown cold. A shiver starting on the side away from her would twitch my shoulders when I tried to repress it; she would frown and unconsciously draw my arm tighter. No one had switched the kitchen light off. On Margaret's foreshortened upper lip there seemed to be two pencil marks; the length of wrist my badly fitting sleeve exposed looked pale and naked against the spiralling down of the smaller arm held beneath it.

Outside, on the street the house faced, there was no motion. Only once did a car go by: around five o'clock, with twin mufflers, the radio on and a boy yelling. Neil and the girl murmured together incessantly; some of what they said I could overhear.

"No. Which?" she asked.

"I don't care."

"Wouldn't you want a boy?"

"I'd be happy whatever I got."

"I know, but which would you *rather* have? Don't men want boys?"

"I don't care. You."

Somewhat later, Mohn's truck passed on the other side of the street. The milkman, well bundled, sat behind headlights in a warm orange volume the size of a phone booth, steering one-handed and smoking a cigar that he set on the edge of the dashboard when, his wire carrier vibrant, he ran out of the truck with bottles. His passing led Neil to decide the time had come. Margaret woke up frightened of her father; we hissed our farewells and thanks to her quickly. Neil dropped the other girl off at her house, a few blocks away; he knew where it was. Sometime during that night I must have seen this girl's face, but I have no memory of it. She is always behind a magazine or in the dark or with her back turned. Neil married her years later, I know, but after we arrived in Chicago I never saw him again either.

A pre-dawn light touched the clouds above the black slate roofs as, with a few other cars, we drove through Alton. The moon-sized clock of a beer billboard said ten after six. Olinger was deathly still. The air brightened as we moved along the highway; the glowing wall of my home hung above the woods as we rounded the long curve by the Mennonite dairy. With a .22 I could have had a pane of my parents' bedroom window, and they were dreaming I was in Indiana. My grandfather would be up, stamping around in the kitchen for my grandmother to make him breakfast, or outside, walking to see if any ice had formed on the brook. For an instant I genuinely feared he might hail me from the peak of the barn roof. Then trees interceded and we were safe in a landscape where no one cared about us.

At the entrance to the Turnpike Neil did a strange thing: he stopped the car and had me take the wheel. He had never trusted me to drive his father's car before, as if my not knowing all about crankshafts and carburetors the way he did handicapped my competence to steer. But now he was quite complacent. He hunched in his gabardine suit under an old mackinaw and leaned his head against the metal of the window frame and soon was asleep. We crossed the Susquehanna on a long smooth bridge below Harrisburg, then began climbing toward the Alleghenies. In the mountains there was snow, a dry dusting like sand, that waved back and forth on the road surface. Farther along there had been a fresh fall that night, about two inches, and the plows had not yet cleared all the lanes. I was passing a Sunoco truck on a high curve when without warning the scraped section gave out and I realized I might skid into the fence if not over the edge. The radio was singing "Carpets of clover, I'll lay right at your feet," and the speedometer said eighty. Nothing happened; the Chrysler stayed firm in the snow and Neil slept through the danger, his face turned skyward and his breath struggling in his nose. It was the first time I heard a contemporary of mine snore.

When we came into tunnel country the flicker and hollow amplification stirred Neil awake. He sat up, the mackinaw dropping to his lap, and lit a cigarette. A second after the scratch of his match occurred the moment of which each following moment was a slight diminution, as we made the long irregular descent toward Pittsburgh. There were many reasons for my feeling so happy. We were on our way. I had seen a dawn. This far, Neil could appreciate, I had brought us safely. Ahead, a girl waited who, if I asked, would marry me, but first there was a vast trip: many hours and towns interceded between me and that encounter. There was the quality of the ten a.m. sunlight as it existed in the air ahead of the windshield, filtered by the thin overcast, blessing irresponsibility – you felt you could slice forever through such a cool pure element – and springing, by implying how high these hills had become, a widespreading pride: Pennsylvania, your state – as if you had made your life. And there was knowing that twice since midnight a person had trusted me enough to fall asleep beside me.

# THE PERSISTENCE
OF DESIRE

PENNYPACKER'S OFFICE still smelled of linoleum, a clean, sad scent that seemed to lift from the checkerboard floor in squares of alternating intensity; this pattern had given Clyde as a boy a funny nervous feeling of intersection, and now he stood crisscrossed by a double sense of himself, his present identity extending down from Massachusetts to meet his disconsolate youth in Pennsylvania, projected upward from a distance of years. The enlarged, tinted photograph of a lake in the Canadian wilderness still covered one whole wall, and the walnut-stained chairs and benches continued their vague impersonation of the Shaker manner. The one new thing, set squarely on an orange end table, was a compact black clock constructed like a speedometer; it showed in arabic numerals the present minute – 1:28 – and coiled invisibly in its works the two infinities of past and future. Clyde was early; the waiting room was empty. He sat down on a chair opposite the clock. Already it was 1:29, and while he watched, the digits slipped again: another drop into the brimming void. He glanced around for the comfort of a clock with a face and gracious, gradual hands. A stopped grandfather matched the other imitation antiques. He opened a magazine and immediately read, "Science reveals that the cells of the normal human body are replaced *in toto* every seven years."

The top half of a Dutch door at the other end of the room opened, and, framed in the square, Pennypacker's secretary turned the bright disc of her face toward him. "Mr. Behn?" she asked in a chiming voice. "Dr. Pennypacker will be back from lunch in a minute." She vanished backward into the maze of little rooms where Pennypacker, an eye, ear, nose, and throat man, had arranged his fabulous equipment. Through the bay window Clyde could see traffic, gayer in color than he remembered, hustle down Grand Avenue. On the sidewalk, haltered girls identical in all but name with girls he had known strolled past in twos and threes. Small-town perennials, they moved rather mournfully under their burdens of bloom. In the opposite direction packs of the opposite sex carried baseball mitts.

Clyde became so lonely watching his old street that when, with a sucking exclamation, the door from the vestibule opened, he looked up gratefully, certain that the person, this being his home town, would be a friend. When he saw who it was, although every cell in his body had been replaced since he had last seen her, his hands jerked in his lap and blood bounded against his skin.

"Clyde Behn," she pronounced, with a matronly and patronizing yet frightened finality, as if he were a child and these words the moral of a story.

"Janet." He awkwardly rose from his chair and crouched, not so much in courtesy as to relieve the pressure on his heart.

"Whatever brings you back to these parts?" She was taking the pose that she was just anyone who once knew him.

He slumped back. "I'm always coming back. It's just you've never been here."

"Well, I've" – she seated herself on an orange bench and crossed her plump legs cockily – "been in Germany with my husband."

"He was in the Air Force."

"Yes." It startled her a little that he knew.

"And he's out now?" Clyde had never met him, but, having now seen Janet again, he felt he knew him well – a slight, literal fellow, to judge from the shallowness of the marks he had left on her. He would wear eyebrow-style glasses, be a griper, have some not-quite-negotiable talent, like playing the clarinet or drawing political cartoons, and now be starting up a drab avenue of business. Selling insurance, most likely. Poor Janet, Clyde felt; except for the interval of himself – his splendid, perishable self – she would never see the light. Yet she had retained her beautiful calm, an unsleeping tranquillity marked by that pretty little lavender puffiness below the eyes. And either she had grown slimmer or he had grown more tolerant of fat. Her thick ankles and the general *obstinacy* of her flesh used to goad him into being cruel.

"Yes." Her voice indicated that she had withdrawn; perhaps some ugliness of their last parting had recurred to her.

"I was 4-F." He was ashamed of this, and his confessing it, though she seemed unaware of the change, turned their talk inward. "A peacetime slacker," he went on, "what could be more ignoble?"

She was quiet a while, then asked, "How many children do you have?"

"Two. Age three and one. A girl and a boy; very symmetrical. Do you" – he blushed lightly, and brushed at his forehead to hide it – "have any?"

"No, we thought it wouldn't be fair, until we were more fixed."

Now the quiet moment was his to hold; she had matched him failing for failing. She recrossed her legs, and in a quaint strained way smiled.

"I'm trying to remember," he admitted, "the last time we saw each other. I can't remember how we broke up."

"I can't either," she said. "It happened so often."

Clyde wondered if with that sarcasm she intended to fetch his eyes to the brink of tears. Probably not; premeditation had never been much of a weapon for her, though she had tried to learn it from him.

He moved across the linoleum to sit on the bench beside her. "I can't tell you," he said, "how much, of all the people in this town, you were the one I wanted to see." It was foolish, but he had prepared it to say, in case he ever saw her again.

"Why?" This was more like her: blunt, pucker-lipped curiosity. He had forgotten it.

"Well, hell. Any number of reasons. I wanted to say something."

"What?"

"Well, that if I hurt you it was stupidity, because I was young. I've often wondered since if I did, because it seems now that you were the only person outside my family who ever, actually, *liked* me."

"Did I?"

"If you think by doing nothing but asking monosyllabic questions you're making an effect, you're wrong."

She averted her face, leaving, in a sense, only her body – the pale, columnar breadth of arm, the freckled crescent of shoulder muscle under the cotton strap of her summer dress – with him. "You're the one who's making effects." It was such a wan, senseless thing to say to defend herself; Clyde, virtually paralyzed by so heavy an injection of love, touched her arm icily.

With a quickness that suggested she had foreseen this, she got up and went to the table by the bay window, where rows of overlapping magazines were laid. She bowed her head to their titles, the nape of her neck in shadow beneath a half-collapsed bun. She had always had trouble keeping her hair pinned.

Clyde was blushing intensely. "Is your husband working around here?"

"He's looking for work." That she kept her back turned while saying this gave him hope.

"Mr. Behn?" The petite secretary-nurse, switching like a pendulum, led him back through the sanctums and motioned for him to sit in a high hinged chair padded with black leather. Pennypacker's equipment had always made him nervous; tons of it were marshalled through the rooms. A complex tree of tubes and lenses leaned over his left shoulder, and by his right elbow a porcelain basin was cupped expectantly. An eye chart crisply stated gibberish. In time Pennypacker himself appeared: a tall, stooped man with mottled cheekbones and an air of suppressed anger.

"Now what's the trouble, Clyde?"

"It's nothing; I mean it's very little," Clyde began, laughing inappropriately. During his adolescence he had developed a joking familiarity with his dentist and his regular doctor, but he had never become cozy with Pennypacker, who remained, what he had seemed at first, an aloof administrator of expensive humiliations. He had made Clyde wear glasses when he was in the third grade. Later, he annually cleaned, with a shrill push of hot water, wax from Clyde's ears, and once had thrust two copper straws up Clyde's nostrils in a futile attempt to purge his sinuses. Clyde always felt unworthy of Pennypacker – felt himself to be a dirty conduit balking the smooth onward flow of the doctor's reputation and apparatus. He blushed to mention his latest trivial stoppage. "It's just that for over two months I've had this eyelid that twitters and it makes it difficult to think."

Pennypacker drew little circles with a pencil-sized flash-light in front of Clyde's right eye.

"It's the left lid," Clyde said, without daring to turn his head. "I went to a doctor up where I live, and he said it was like a rattle in the fender and there was nothing to do. He said it would go away, but it didn't and didn't, so I had my mother make an appointment for when I came down here to visit."

Pennypacker moved to the left eye and drew even closer. The distance between the doctor's eyes and the corners of his mouth was very long; the emotional impression of his face close up was like that of those first photographs taken from rockets, in which the earth's curvature was made apparent. "How do you like being in your home territory?" Pennypacker asked.

"Fine."

"Seem a little strange to you?"

The question itself seemed strange. "A little."

"Mm. That's interesting."

"About the eye, there were two things I thought," Clyde said. "One was, I got some glasses made in Massachusetts by a man nobody else ever went to, and I thought his prescription might be faulty. His equipment seemed so ancient and kind of full of cobwebs – like a Dürer print." He never could decide how cultured Pennypacker was; the Canadian lake argued against it, but he was county-famous in his trade, in a county where doctors were as high as the intellectual scale went.

The flashlight, a tepid sun girdled by a grid of optical circles behind which Pennypacker's face loomed dim and colorless, came right to the skin of Clyde's eye, and the vague face lurched forward angrily, and Clyde, blind in a world of light, feared that Pennypacker was inspecting the floor of his soul. Paralyzed by panic, he breathed, "The other was that something might be in it. At night it feels as if there's a tiny speck deep in under the lid."

Pennypacker reared back and insolently raked the light back and forth across Clyde's face. "How long have you had this flaky stuff on your lids?"

The insult startled Clyde. "Is there any?"

"How long have you had it?"

"Some mornings I notice little grains like salt that I thought were what I used to call sleepy-dust –"

"This isn't sleepy-dust," the doctor said. He repeated, "This isn't sleepy-dust." Clyde started to smile at what he took to be kidding of his babyish vocabulary, but Penny-packer cut him short with "Cases of this can lead to loss of the eyelashes."

"Really?" Clyde was vain of his lashes, which in his boy-hood had been exceptionally long, giving his face the alert and tender look of a girl's. "Do you think it's the reason for the tic?" He imagined his face with the lids bald and the lashes lying scattered on his cheeks like insect legs. "What can I do?"

"Are you using your eyes a great deal?"

"Some. No more than I ever did."

Pennypacker's hands, blue after Clyde's dazzlement, lifted an intensely brown bottle from a drawer. "It may be bacteria, it may be allergy; when you leave I'll give you something that should knock it out either way. Do you follow me? Now, Clyde" – his voice became murmurous and consolatory as he placed a cupped hand, rigid as an electrode, on the top of Clyde's head – "I'm going to put some drops in your eyes so we can check the prescription of the glasses you bought in Massachusetts."

Clyde didn't remember that the drops stung so; he gasped outright and wept while Pennypacker held the lids apart with his fingers and worked them gently open and shut, as if he were playing with snapdragons. Pennypacker set preposterously small, circular dark-brown glasses on Clyde's face and in exchange took away the stylish horn-rims Clyde had kept in his pocket. It was Pennypacker's method to fill his little rooms with waiting patients and wander from one to another like a dungeon-keeper.

Clyde heard, far off, the secretary's voice tinkle, and, amplified by the hollow hall, Pennypacker's rumble in welcome and Janet's respond. The one word "headaches," petulantly emphasized, stood up in her answer. Then a door was shut. Silence.

Clyde admired how matter-of-fact she had sounded. He had always admired this competence in her, her authority in the world peripheral to the world of love, in which she was so docile. He remembered how she could face up to waitresses and teachers and how she would bluff her mother when this vigilant woman unexpectedly entered the screened porch where they were supposed to be playing cribbage. Potted elephant plants sat in the corners of the porch like faithful dwarfs; robins had built a nest in the lilac outside, inches from the screen. It had been taken as an omen, a blessing, when, one evening, their being on the glider no longer distressed the robins.

The wallpaper he saw through the open door seemed as distinct as ever. Unlike, say, the effects of Novocain, the dilation of pupils is impalpable. He held his fingernails close to his nose and was unable to distinguish the cuticles. He touched the sides of his nose, where tears had left trails. He looked at his fingers again, and they seemed fuzzier. He couldn't see his fingerprint whorls. The threads of his shirt had melted into an elusive liquid surface.

A door opened and closed, and another patient was ushered into a consulting room and imprisoned by Penny-packer. Janet's footsteps had not mingled with the others. Without ever quite sacrificing his reputation for good behavior, Clyde in high school had become fairly bold in heckling teachers he considered stupid or unjust. He got out of his chair, looked down the hall to where a white splinter of secretary showed, and quickly walked past a closed door to one ajar. His blood told him, *This one.*

Janet was sitting in a chair as upright as the one he had left, a two-pronged comb in her mouth, her back arched, and her arms up, bundling her hair. As he slipped around the door, she plucked the comb from between her teeth and laughed at him. He saw in a little rimless mirror cocked above her head his own head, grimacing with stealth and grotesquely costumed in glasses like two chocolate coins, and appreciated her laughter, though it didn't fit with what he had prepared to say. He said it anyway: "Janet, are you happy?"

She rose with a practical face and walked past him and clicked the door shut. As she stood facing it, listening for a reaction from outside, he gathered her hair in his hand and lifted it from the nape of her neck, which he had expected to find in shadow but which was instead, to his distended eyes, bright as a candle. He clumsily put his lips to it.

"Don't you love your wife?" she asked.

"Incredibly much," he murmured into the fine neck-down.

She moved off, leaving him leaning awkwardly, and in front of the mirror smoothed her hair away from her ears. She sat down again, crossing her wrists in her lap.

"I just got told my eyelashes are going to fall out," Clyde said.

"Your pretty lashes," she said somberly.

"Why do you hate me?"

"Shh. I don't hate you now."

"But you did once."

"No, I did *not* once. Clyde, what *is* this bother? What are you after?"

"Son of a bitch, so I'm a bother. I knew it. You've just forgotten, all the time I've been remembering; you're so *damn* dense. I come in here a bundle of pain to tell you I'm sorry and I want you to be happy, and all I get is the back of your neck." Affected by what had happened to his eyes, his tongue had loosened, pouring out impressions; with culminating incoherence he dropped to his knees beside her chair, wondering if the thump would bring Pennypacker. "I must see you again," he blurted.

"Shh."

"I come back here and the only person who was ever pleasant to me I discover I maltreated so much she hates me."

"Clyde," she said, "you didn't maltreat me. You were a sweet boy to me."

Straightening up on his knees, he fumbled his fingers around the hem of the neck of her dress and pulled it out and looked down into the blurred cavity between her breasts. He had a remembrance of her freckles going down from her shoulders into her bathing suit. His glasses hit her cheek.

She stabbed the back of his hand with the points of her comb and he got to his feet, rearing high into a new, less sorrowful atmosphere. "When?" he asked, short of breath.

"No," she said.

"What's your married name?"

"Clyde, I thought you were successful. I thought you had beautiful children. Aren't you happy?"

"I am, I am; but" – the rest was so purely inspired its utterance only grazed his lips – "happiness isn't everything."

Footsteps ticked down the hall, toward their door, past it. Fear emptied his chest, yet with an excellent imitation of his old high-school flippancy he blew her a kiss, waited, opened the door, and whirled through it. His hand had left the knob when the secretary, emerging from the room where he should have been, confronted him in the linoleum-smelling hall. "Where could I get a drink of water?" he asked plaintively, assuming the hunch and whine of a blind beggar. In truth, he had, without knowing it, become thirsty.

"Once a year I pass through your territory," Pennypacker intoned as he slipped a growing weight of lenses into the apparatus on Clyde's nose. He had returned to Clyde more relaxed and chatty, now that all his little rooms were full. Clyde had tried to figure out from the pattern of noise if Janet had been dismissed. He believed she had. The thought made his eyelid throb. He didn't even know her married name. "Down the Turnpike," Pennypacker droned on, while his face flickered in and out of focus, "up the New Jersey Pike, over the George Washington Bridge, up the Saw Mill, then Route 7 all the way to Lake Champlain. To hunt the big bass. There's an experience for you."

"I notice you have a new clock in your waiting room."

"That's a Christmas present from the Alton Optical Company. Can you read that line?"

"H, L, F, Y, T, something that's either an S or an E –"

"K," Pennypacker said without looking. The poor devil, he had all those letters memorized, all that gibberish – abruptly, Clyde wanted to love him. The oculist altered one lens. "Is it better this way? . . . Or this way?"

At the end of the examination, Pennypacker said, "Though the man's equipment was dusty, he gave you a good prescription. In your right eye the axis of astigmatism has rotated several degrees, which is corrected in the lenses. If you have been experiencing a sense of strain, part of the reason, Clyde, is that these heavy tortoiseshell frames are slipping down on your nose and giving you a prismatic effect. For a firm fit you should have metal frames, with adjustable nose pads."

"They leave such ugly dents on the sides of your nose."

"You should have them. Your bridge, you see" – he tapped his own – "is recessed. It takes a regular face to support un-articulated frames. Do you wear your glasses all the time?"

"For the movies and reading. When I got them in the third grade you told me that was all I needed them for."

"You should wear them all the time."

"Really? Even just for walking around?"

"All the time, yes. You have middle-aged eyes."

Pennypacker gave him a little plastic squeeze bottle of drops. "That is for the fungus on your lids."

"Fungus? There's a brutal thought. Well, will it cure the tic?"

Pennypacker impatiently snapped, "The tic is caused by muscular fatigue."

Thus Clyde was dismissed into a tainted world where things evaded his focus. He went down the hall in his sunglasses and was told by the secretary that he would receive a bill. The waiting room was full now, mostly with downcast old men and myopic children gnawing at their mothers. From out of this crowd a ripe young woman arose and came against his chest, and Clyde, included in the close aroma her hair and skin gave off, felt weak and broad and grand, like a declining rose. Janet tucked a folded note into the pocket of his shirt and said conversationally, "He's waiting outside in the car."

The neutral, ominous "he" opened wide a conspiracy Clyde instantly entered. He stayed behind a minute, to give her time to get away. Ringed by the judging eyes of the young and old, he felt like an actor snug behind the blinding protection of the footlights; he squinted prolongedly at the speedometer-clock, which, like a letter delivered on the stage, in fact was blank. Then, smiling ironically toward both sides, he left the waiting room, coming into Pennypacker's entrance hall, a cubicle equipped with a stucco umbrella stand and a red rubber mat saying, in letters so large he could read them, WALK IN.

He had not expected to be unable to read her note. He held it at arm's length and slowly brought it toward his face, wiggling it in the light from outdoors. Though he did this several times, it didn't yield even the simplest word, just wet blue specks. Under the specks, however, in their intensity and disposition, he believed he could make out the handwriting – slanted, open, unoriginal – familiar to him from other notes received long ago. This glimpse, through the skin of the paper, of Janet's old self quickened and sweetened his desire more than touching her had. He tucked the note back into his shirt pocket and its stiffness there made a shield for his heart. In this armor he stepped into the familiar street. The maples, macadam, shadows, houses, cars were to his violated eyes as brilliant as a scene remembered; he became a child again in this town, where life was a distant adventure, a rumor, an always imminent joy.

# THE BLESSED MAN
OF BOSTON,
MY GRANDMOTHER'S
THIMBLE, AND
FANNING ISLAND

I SAW HIM only for a moment, and that was years ago. Boston had been beaten by the White Sox. It was a night game, and when it was over, as the crowd, including myself and my friends, pushed with that suppressed Occidental panic up the aisles toward the exit ramps, he, like the heavy pebble of gold that is not washed from the pan, was revealed, sitting alone, immobile and smiling, among the green seats. He was an old Chinese man, solidly fat, like a Chevrolet dealer, and he wore faded black trousers and a white shirt whose sleeves were rolled up. He sat with one arm up on the back of the seat beside him and smiled out toward the field, where the ground crew was unfurling the tarp across the foreshortened clay diamond and the outfield under the arc lights looked as brilliant and flat as a pool-table felt. And it flashed upon me, as I glimpsed this man sitting alone and unperturbed among the drained seats, that here was the happy man, the man of unceasing and effortless blessing. I thought then to write a novel, an immense book, about him, recounting his every move, his every meal, every play, pitch, and hesitation of every ball game he attended, the number of every house he passed as he walked Boston's three-decker slums, the exact position and shape of every cracked and flaking spot on the doorways, the precise sheen and rust of every floriated and convoluted fancy of ironwork that drifted by his legs, the chalk marks, the bricks (purple-tinted, ochre-smeared, red), the constellations of lint and stain in his tiny bachelor's room (green walls, painted pipes coughing with steam, telephone wiring stapled along the baseboard), the never precisely duplicated curl of the smoke off his rice, the strokes of sound composing the hatchings of noise at his back, every stifled cry, every sizzle of a defective neon-sign connection, every distant plane and train, every roller-skate scratch, everything: all set sequentially down with the bald simplicity of a litany, thousands upon thousands of pages, ecstatically uneventful, divinely and defiantly dull.

But we would-be novelists have a reach as shallow as our skins. We walk through volumes of the unexpressed and like snails leave behind a faint thread excreted out of ourselves. From the dew of the few flakes that melt on our faces we cannot reconstruct the snowstorm.

The other night I stumbled downstairs in the dark and kicked my wife's sewing basket from the halfway landing. Needles, spools, buttons, and patches scattered. In gathering the things up, I came upon my grandmother's thimble. For a second I did not know what it was; a stemless chalice of silver weighing a fraction of an ounce had come into my fingers. Then I knew, and the valves of time parted, and after an interval of years my grandmother was upon me again, and it seemed incumbent upon me, necessary and holy, to tell how once there had been a woman who now was no more, how she had been born and lived in a world that had ceased to exist, though its mementos were all about us; how her thimble had been fashioned as if in a magical grotto in the black mountain of time, by workmen dwarfed by remoteness, in a vanished workshop now no larger than the thimble itself and like it soon doomed, as if by geological pressures, to be crushed out of shape. O Lord, bless these poor paragraphs, that would do in their vile ignorance Your work of resurrection.

The thimble was her wedding present to me and my wife. I was her only grandchild. At the time I was married, she was in her late seventies, crippled and enfeebled. She had fought a long battle with Parkinson's disease; in my earliest memories of her she is touched with it. Her fingers and back are bent; there is a tremble about her as she moves through the dark, odd-shaped rooms of our house in the town where I was born. Crouched in the hall outside my grandparents' room – which I never entered – I can hear her voice, in a whispering mutter that pierces the wall with little snapping stabs, irritably answer a question that my grandfather had asked inaudibly. It is strange: out of their room, he speaks louder. When she bends over me, I smell a mixture of must, something like cough medicine, and old cloth permeated with dried sunlight. In my childhood she was strong, endowed with possessions and resources. By the time I married, she had become so weak only her piercing will carried her up and down the stairs of the little country house to which we had moved – the very house where she had lived as a bride. She spoke with great difficulty; she would hang impaled in the middle of a sentence, at a loss for the word, her watery eyes and wild white hair transfixed. She had no possessions. Except for her clothes and her bed, the elegant silver thimble – a gift from her father, inscribed with her maiden initials – was her last property, and she gave it to us.

In those days each departure from her I thought was the last. When I left to be married, I did not expect to see her alive again. But when, at the end of the summer, my wife and I returned, it was my grandfather, and not she, who had died. He had died minutes before we arrived. His body lay on the floor of their bedroom, his mouth a small black triangle in a face withered beyond recognition. The room was dimly lit by the warm glow of a kerosene lamp. I was afraid of his body; it surprised me that she did not seem to be. I was afraid that his body would move. I called "Grandpa" in an experimental whisper and flinched in fear of an answer.

My grandmother sat on the edge of the bed, dazed, smiling slightly to greet me. She was confused, like a craftsman who looks up after a long period of concentration. The sanest of old men, my grandfather had on his last day lost his mind. He had bellowed; she had struggled to restrain him. He thought the bed was on fire and sprang from it; she clung to him, and in their fall to the floor he died. But not quite. My mother rushed up the stairs and cried, "What are you doing?"

"Why, we're on the floor," her father told her with level sarcasm, and his heart stopped.

My father met our headlights on the lawn; he was panting. "Jesus," he said to me, "you've come at a funny time; we think Pop's died." My parents-in-law were with us; my wife's father, a surgeon, an intimate of death, went upstairs to the body. He came down, smiling, and said that there was no pulse, though the wrist was still warm. Then, when I went upstairs, I saw my grandmother smiling in much the same abstracted, considerate way as he.

She sat, worn and cleansed by her struggle, on the edge of the bed with two hollows. She was a little woman informed by a disproportionate strength. Carrying her husband through his death had been her last great effort. From that moment on, her will tried to arrange itself for defeat, and its power of resistance became an inconvenience to her. I hugged her quickly, afraid too of her body, which had so lately embraced the one on the floor. My mother, behind me, asked her if she wanted to come downstairs with the others. My grandmother refused, saying, "A little while yet," and making a tremulous impatient motion of explanation or dismissal.

She knew, perhaps, what I was shocked to discover when, descending the steps with trembling knees, and tingling all over as if from a bath, I went downstairs: that we have no gestures adequate to answer the imperious gestures of nature. Among deaf mountains human life pursues a comic low road. The sherry that my mother had purchased toward our arrival was served; the wait for the undertaker became overlaid with a subdued version of the party she had meant to have. My father-in-law with a chilling professional finesse carved the cold ham; my mother, tautly calm, as if at the center of contradictory tensions, made one or two of her witticisms; my father's telephone conversation with our Lutheran minister was as bewildered and bewildering as his conversations with this young man always were. Without knowing what I had expected instead, I was amazed; the chatter seemed to become unbearably loud and I blurted, thinking of my grandmother listening above our heads, "Why can't you let the old man rest?" My mother looked at me in startled reproval, and I felt again the security of being her clever but inexperienced boy; there were things I didn't understand.

The minister came with a drawn white face that cracked in relief at finding laughter in the house. At church softball he had broken his ankle sliding into second base, and limped still. His prayers seemed to chip pieces from our hearts and float them away. The undertaker's men, droll wooden figures like the hangmen of old, came and trundled the body out the door. Thus, as if through a series of pressure locks, we were rescued from the presence of death.

My grandmother did not attend the funeral. She was wise, for the Masons made it ridiculous with their occult presumption. My grandmother, whose love of activity had been intense, stayed inside the house, and more and more in bed.

When my wife and I went away again – I had a year of college left – I said goodbye to her in my heart. But when we returned at Christmas, she was alive, and she was alive in June, though by now completely bedridden.

Blindly her will gave battle. My grandfather had been a vigorous booster of exercise as the key to longevity. Obeying, perhaps, an echo of her husband's voice, my grandmother would ask to be lifted by her hands into a sitting position, and then lowered, and lifted again, until the person doing it for her lost patience and in exasperation quit. She liked company, though almost all power of speech had forsaken her. "Up. Up," that fierce and plaintive request, was all I could understand. We knew that the disease touched only her tongue; that in that wordless, glaring head the same alert and appetitive mind lived. But a mind shorn of agency ceases to exist in our world, and we would speak together in her room as if it were empty. Certain now that this was my last time with her – my wife and I were going to England for a year – I spent some summer afternoons in my grandmother's room. I knew she could hear, but we had never spoken much to each other, so I would read or write in silence. I remember sitting in the rocking chair at the foot of the bed, near the spot where my grandfather's body had lain that night in warm lamplight, and writing, while the sun streamed in through the geraniums on the windowsill, a piece of light verse about what I imagined the sea voyage I was soon to take would be like.

> That line is the horizon line.
> The blue above it is divine.
> The blue below it is marine.
> Sometimes the blue below is green.

Reading this stanza now, I see, as if over the edge of the paper, my grandmother's nostrils. Her head was sunk fore-shortened in the pillow. Decrepitude pressed unevenly on her body, twisted it out of symmetry; one nostril was squeezed into teardrop-shape, and the other was a round black hole through which she seized the air. The whole delicate frame of her existence seemed suspended from this final hungry aperture, the size of a dime, through which her life was sustained.

In England I hesitated to tear open each letter from home, for fear it would contain the news of her death. But, as if preserved in the unreality of those days that passed without weight on an island whose afternoon was our morning and whose morning was our night, she survived, and was there when we returned. We had had a baby girl. We put the child, too young to creep, on my grandmother's bed beside the hump of her legs, so that for an interval four generations were gathered in one room, and without moving her head my grandmother could see her entire progeny: my mother, myself, and my daughter. Later, at the old woman's funeral, my child, by then alert to things around her, smiled and from my arms stretched her hand toward the drained and painted body in the casket, perhaps in some faint way familiar.

My grandmother had died, finally, when I was far away, in Boston. I was at a party; it was a Saturday night. I went to the phone with a cigarette in my hand and Cointreau on my breath; my mother, her voice miniature with distance, began the conversation with the two words, "Grammy went." They had found her dead in the morning and had not been able to reach me until now. It was, of course, a blessing; my mother's health had been nearly broken by nursing her own mother. Now we were all released. I returned to the party and told my news, which was received respectfully; it was a small party, of old friends. But the party spirit cannot be suppressed a whole evening, and when it revived I suppose I joined it. I vowed, groping for some fitness, for the commensurate gesture, to go to a Lutheran church the next morning. But when Sunday morning came, I slept late, and the vow seemed a troublesome whim. I did not go.

*I did not go.* This refusal seems to be a face at that party and I am about to quarrel with it, but other memories come and touch my elbow and lead me away.

When we were all still alive, the five of us in that kerosene-lit house, on Friday and Saturday nights, at an hour when in the spring and summer there was still abundant light in the air, I would set out in my father's car for town, where my friends lived. I had, by moving ten miles away, at last acquired friends: an illustration of that strange law whereby, like Orpheus leading Eurydice, we achieve our desire by turning our back on it. I had even gained a girl, so that the vibrations were as sexual as social that made me jangle with anticipation as I clowned in front of the mirror in our kitchen, shaving from a basin of stove-heated water, combing my hair with a dripping comb, adjusting my reflection in the mirror until I had achieved just that electric angle from which my face seemed beautiful and everlastingly, by the very volumes of air and sky and grass that lay mutely banked about our home, beloved. My grandmother would hover near me, watching fearfully, as she had when I was a child, afraid that I would fall from a tree. Delirious, humming, I would swoop and lift her, lift her like a child, crooking one arm under her knees and cupping the other behind her back. Exultant in my height, my strength, I would lift that frail brittle body weighing perhaps a hundred pounds and twirl with it in my arms while the rest of the family watched with startled smiles of alarm. Had I stumbled, or dropped her, I might have broken her back, but my joy always proved a secure cradle. And whatever irony was in the impulse, whatever implicit contrast between this ancient husk, scarcely female, and the pliant, warm girl I would embrace before the evening was done, direct delight flooded away: I was carrying her who had carried me, I was giving my past a dance, I had lifted the anxious caretaker of my childhood from the floor, I was bringing her with my boldness to the edge of danger, from which she had always sought to guard me.

There is a photograph of my grandmother and me at the side of the first house. There is snow on the ground. The brick walk has been cleared. I am in a snowsuit, and its bulk makes my walking doubly clumsy. We are both of us dark against the snow and the white brick wall of the house. I am unsteady; my grandmother's black shape bends over me with a predatory solicitude, holding one of my hands in a hand that has already become, under the metamorphosis of her disease, a little clawlike. She was worried that I would fall, that I would not eat enough, that the bigger boys of the neighborhood would harm me, that a cold would strangle me; and her fears were not foolish. There *was* danger in that kind house. Tigers of temper lurked beneath the furniture, and shadows of despair followed my father to the door and flattened themselves against the windows as he walked down the shaded street alone.

I remember watching my mother iron in the dining room. Suddenly her hand jumps to her jaw; her face goes white; shock unfocuses her eyes. Her teeth had given her a twinge that started tears flowing down her cheeks as she resumed ironing. I must have cried out, for she smiled at my face. I told her she must go to the dentist, and returned to my coloring book. The comforting aroma of heated cloth folded over the glimpsed spark of pain. Now around that cold spark, isolated in memory, the air of that house crystallizes: our neglected teeth, our poor and starchy diet, our worn floors, our musty and haunted halls. I sit on the carpet – which under the dining table had retained its fresh nap and seemed to me jungle-grass – and my mother stands at the ironing board, and around us, like hieroglyphs haloing the rigid figures of a tomb mural, are the simple shapes of the other three: my grandfather a pyramid sitting rereading the newspaper in the dwindling light of the front parlor, my father a forked stick striding somewhere in the town, my grandmother, above us in her room or behind us in the kitchen, a crescent bent into some chore. As long as her body permitted, she worked.

The night we moved, my mother and I came through the wet black grass around the edge of the sandstone farmhouse and saw, framed in the doorway, close to us yet far away, like a woman in a Vermeer, my grandmother reaching up with a trembling match to touch the wick of a lamp on the high kitchen mantel. My mother's voice, in recalling that moment to me years later, broke as she added, "She was always doing things like that." Like lighting a lamp. Always lighting a lamp.

And through that "always" I fall into the volume of time that preceded my birth, where my grandmother is a figure of history made deceptively tangible by her persistence into my days. She was the youngest of a dozen children, all of whom, remarkably in that mortal era, lived to maturity. She was the baby, her father's favorite and her brothers' darling. Toward the end of her life, when hallucinations began to walk through the walls of her room and stand silently in the corners, her brothers, all of whom she had long outlived, became again vivid to her. I became one of them; she would ask for me with Pete's name. He was her youngest brother, her own favorite. His brown photograph, mounted on stiff cardboard stamped with gold scrolls, had been set up on the table beside her bed. He displayed a hook nose and the dandified hauteur of a rural buck braced to have his picture taken. Like the eyes of an icon, his snapping black eyes – alone in the photograph unfaded – overlooked her deathbed.

I believe her first language was Pennsylvania German. As some parents speak secrets in French in front of the children, my grandparents used this dialect on my mother. Only two words have descended to me – *ferhuttled* and *dopich*, respectively meaning "confused" and "lethargic." They were frequent words with my grandmother; it is the way other people must have looked to her. Shaped like a sickle, her life whipped through grasses of confusion and lethargy that in a summer month grew up again as tall as before.

As with the blessed man of Boston, I should here provide a catalogue of her existence: her marriage to a man ten years older, the torment of her one childbirth, the eddies of fortune that contained her constant labor. The fields, the hired men, the horses, the stones of the barn and the fireplace, the three-mile inns on the road to market. The birth of my mother: the lamplight, the simmering water, the buggy clattering for the tipsy doctor, fear like a transparent paste on the ceiling, the hours of pain piled higher and higher – my grandmother was a little woman, and the baby was large. Her size at the outset my mother felt as an insult ineradicably delivered to the woman who bore her, the first of a thousand painful failures to do the normal thing. But to me, from my remote perspective, in which fable, memory, and blood blend, the point of the story is the survival. Both survived the ordeal. And in the end all my impressions of my grandmother's life turn on the point of her survival.

When we returned to the farm where my mother had been born, my grandmother insisted on fetching the water from the spring. In spite of all our warnings, she would sneak off with the bucket and on her unsteady legs tote it back up the slope of grass, brimful, strangely little of it spilled. One summer day my mother and I were standing at the side of the house. The air was vibrating with the noises of nature, the pressing tremolo of insects and birds. Suddenly my mother's face, as if from a twinge of her teeth, went rapt and white: "Listen!" Before I could listen she ran down the lawn toward the spring, I following, and there we found my grandmother doubled up over the water, hanging, by the pressure of one shoulder, to the sandstone wall that cupped the spring on three sides. The weight of the bucket had pulled her forward; she had thrown herself sideways and, unable to move, had held herself from drowning by sheer adhesion of will until her faint, birdlike whimper for help flew to the attuned ears of her child. Death had to take her while she slept.

She never to my knowledge went outside the boundaries of Pennsylvania. She never saw a movie; I never saw her read. She lived in our nation as a fish lives in the deep sea. One night, when she thought – wrongly – that she was dying, I heard her ask, "Will I be a little debil?" I had never before heard her curiosity range so far. When presented with disagreeable information, she would look stunned, then with a glimmer of a smile say slowly, "Ach, I guess not," wishing the obstacle away as easily as a child.

Of course, I came upon her late, with a child's unknowing way of seeing. No doubt the innocence of my vision of her is my own innocence, her ignorance mine. I am told that in her day she was sophisticated and formidable. She liked fine clothes, good food, nice things. She was one of the first women in the region to drive a car. This automobile, an Overland, spinning down the orange dirt roads of rural valleys now filled with ranch houses and Philadelphia commuters, recedes into a landscape and a woman whom I must imagine, a woman who is not my grandmother at all.

The initials were K.Z.K. Picking up that thimble, with its crown of stipples like a miniature honeycomb, and its decorative rim of five-petalled flowers tapped into the silver, I felt at my back that night a steep wave about to break over the world and bury us and all our trinkets of survival fathoms down. For I feel that the world is ending, that the mounting mass of people will soon make a blackness in which the glint of this silver will be obliterated; it is this imminent catastrophe that makes it imperative for me to cry now, in the last second when the cry will have meaning, that once there was a woman whom one of the continents in one of its terrains caused to exist. That the land which cast her up was harsher, more sparsely exploited, more fertile than it is now. That she was unique; that she came toward the end of the time when uniqueness was possible. Already identical faces throng the street. She was projected onto my own days by her willed survival; I lived with her and she loved me and I did not understand her, I did not care to. She is gone now because we deserted her; the thimble seems a keepsake pressed into my hand by a forsaken woman as in the company of others I launched out from an island into a wilderness.

Such simplicities bring me to the third of my unwritten stories. It is a simple story, a story of life stripped of the progenitive illusion, perfected out of history: the slam of a door in an empty house. "Let us imagine," Pascal invites us, "a number of men in chains, and all condemned to death. . . ."

Fanning Island is an isolated Pacific island near the equator. It now supports a relay station for the transoceanic

telegraph. When Captain Fanning discovered it, it was uninhabited, but bore signs of habitation: a rectangular foundation of coral blocks, a basalt adze, some bone fishhooks, a few
raised graves containing drilled porpoise teeth and human
bones. All these things were old.

Understand that the Polynesian islands were populated
accidentally, as seed in nature is sown. On the wide waste
of ocean many canoes and praus were blown astray; short
planned voyages were hazardous and extended navigation
was impossible. Some drifted to other populated islands, and
thorns there swallowed them. Some starved on the barren
expanse of the Pacific; some fell southward into Antarctic ice.
Some washed up on atolls with only the rats in the canoes
still alive. A few – a very few; Nature with her mountain
of time plays a spendthrift game – survived to reach an
uninhabited but inhabitable island. When the company of
survivors included fertile women, population took place.
The souls shed by one nation became the seeds of another.
No return was possible. The stars are a far weaker guide than
armchair theorists believe. Accident, here as elsewhere, is the
generating agency beneath the seemingly achieved surface
of things.

What must have happened is this. A company of men in a
large canoe, sailing among the Marquesas, were blown away.
Eventually they were cast up on Fanning Island. They built
a house, fished, and lived. No women were among them, so
their numbers could only diminish. The youngest among
them may have lived for fifty years. The bones of this man
whom no one remained to bury moldered away and vanished. No sign of disaster is found to explain the disappear-
ance of the men. None is needed.

*Qu'on s'imagine un nombre d'hommes dans les chaînes, et
tous condamnés à la mort, dont les uns étant chaque jour égorgés*

*à la vue des autres, ceux qui restent voient leur propre condition
dans celle de leurs semblables, et, se regardant les uns et les autres
avec douleur et sans espérance, attendent à leur tour. C'est
l'image de la condition des hommes.*

— We came from Hiva Oa, and carried pigs and messages
for Nuku Hiva, below the horizon. My father was chief. The
taboo was strong, and we carried no women in the prau.
The wind dropped, and returned from another quarter. The
sea grew too smooth, and lustrous like the inside of a coconut; the southern sky merged with the sea. In the storm there
were lost many pigs and an old man who had seen Nuku
Hiva as a boy. When the sky cleared, it was night, and the
stars were scrambled. At dawn the horizon all around us was
unbroken; we strained to see when the great waves lifted us
high. We sang to the sun, and slept in the shade of the bodies
of the wakeful. The storm had torn away the hut. The cow-
ards infected us. But the singing gave me comfort, and my
father's presence sheltered me. He was the tallest and bravest,
yet was among those first to yield up life. We devoured his
body; his strength passed into me, though I was young.
I long felt the island approaching. It gave the men hope and
gaiety to touch me. The island first seemed a cloud; but
Marheyo saw birds. Our sails were gone, and we paddled
with hands that had lost shape. Our skin shredded in the
water. Our throats had become stuck; we were silent. Two
days and a night it took us to reach the island; at the second
dawn its arms were reaching for us. We saw green bush and
coconut palms above the rock. Before our strengths were
fully revived, Karnoonoo and I fought. Though he had been
a man feared in the village, I won, and killed him, grieving.
We took thought to shelter. We built a house of stone, carv-
ing the soft rock, like ash, with our axes. We harvested fruit
and fish, and learned to make tapa from the strange bark.

We buried our dead. We carved a god from a log of the prau. We made women of one other. I was the youngest; I gave myself to those men whom I desired, the best-natured. It was not always the old who died. Demons of apathy seized Mehivi, the clown, and Kory-Kory, who had tended the god. The horizon seemed always about to speak to us; for what had we been brought here? We lived, and though we saw the others turn cold, and the jaws sink, and the body turn stiff and light like a child's canoe, those who remained were not sure that they would die. We buried them with the amulets we brought from the village. Now I am the last. I buried Marheyo, the three-fingered, a season ago, and at night he speaks to me.

This is the outline; but it would be the days, the evocation of the days … the green days. The tasks, the grass, the weather, the shades of sea and air. Just as a piece of turf torn from a meadow becomes a *gloria* when drawn by Dürer. Details. Details are the giant's fingers. He seizes the stick and strips the bark and shows, burning beneath, the moist white wood of joy. For I thought that this story, fully told, would become without my willing it a happy story, a story full of joy; had my powers been greater, we would know. As it is, you, like me, must take it on faith.

# PACKED DIRT,
# CHURCHGOING,
# A DYING CAT,
# A TRADED CAR

DIFFERENT THINGS move us. I, David Kern, am always affected – reassured, nostalgically pleased, even, as a member of my animal species, made proud – by the sight of bare earth that has been smoothed and packed firm by the passage of human feet. Such spots abound in small towns: the furtive break in the playground fence dignified into a thoroughfare, the trough of dust underneath each swing, the blurred path worn across a wedge of grass, the anonymous little mound or embankment polished by play and strewn with pebbles like the confetti aftermath of a wedding. Such unconsciously humanized intervals of clay, too humble and common even to have a name, remind me of my childhood, when one communes with dirt down among the legs, as it were, of presiding presences. The earth is our playmate then, and the call to supper has a piercing eschatological ring.

The corner where I now live was recently widened so that the cars going back and forth to the summer colony on the Point would not be troubled to slow down. My neighbor's house was sold to the town and wrecked and picked clean by salvagers and finally burned in a great bonfire of old notched beams and splintered clapboards that leaped tree-high throughout one whole winter day's cold drizzle. Then bulldozers, huge and yellow and loud, appeared on the street and began to gnaw, it seemed, at the corner of our house. My third child, a boy not yet two, came running from the window in tearful panic. After I tried to soothe him with

179

an explanation, he followed me through the house sobbing and wailing " 'Sheen! 'Sheen!" while the machines made our rooms shake with the curses of their labor. They mashed my neighbor's foundation stones into the earth and trimmed the levelled lot just as my grandmother used to trim the excess dough from the edge of the pieplate. They brought the curve of the road right to the corner of my property, and the beaten path that does for a sidewalk in front of my home was sheared diagonally by a foot-high cliff.

Last night I was coming back from across the street, fresh from an impromptu civic lamentation with a neighbor at how unsightly, now that the snow was melted, the awkward-shaped vacant lot the bulldozers had left looked, with its high raw embankment gouged by rivulets and littered with old chimney bricks. And soon, we concluded, now that spring was here, it would be bristling with weeds. Crossing from this conversation, I noticed that where my path had been lopped the cliff no longer existed; feet – children's feet, mostly, for mostly children walk in our town – had worn the sharpness away and molded a little ramp by which ascent was easier.

This small modification, this modest work of human erosion, seemed precious to me not only because it recalled, in the slope and set of the dirt, a part of the path that long ago had led down from my parents' back yard to the high-school softball field. It seemed precious because it had been achieved accidentally, and had about it that repose of grace which is beyond willing. We in America have from the beginning been cleaving and baring the earth, attacking, reforming the immensity of nature we were given. We have explored, on behalf of all mankind, this paradox: the more matter is outwardly mastered, the more it overwhelms us in our hearts. Evidence – gaping right-of-ways, acres merci-lessly scraped, bleeding mountains of muddy fill – surrounds us of a war that is incapable of ceasing, and it is good to know that now there are enough of us to exert a counter-force. If craters were to appear in our landscape tomorrow, the next day there would be usable paths threading down the blasted sides. As our sense of God's forested legacy to us dwindles, there grows, in these worn, rubbed, and patted patches, a sense of human legacy – like those feet of statues of saints which have lost their toes to centuries of kisses. One thinks of John Dewey's definition of God as the union of the actual and the ideal.

There was a time when I wondered why more people did not go to church. Taken purely as a human recreation, what could be more delightful, more unexpected than to enter a venerable and lavishly scaled building kept warm and clean for use one or two hours a week and to sit and stand in unison and sing and recite creeds and petitions that are like paths worn smooth in the raw terrain of our hearts? To listen, or not listen, as a poorly paid but resplendently robed man strives to console us with scraps of ancient epistles and halting accounts, hopelessly compromised by words, of those intimations of divine joy that are like pain in that, their instant gone, the mind cannot remember or believe them; to witness the windows donated by departed patrons and the altar flowers arranged by withdrawn hands and the whole considered spectacle lustrous beneath its patina of long use; to pay, for all this, no more than we are moved to give – surely in all democracy there is nothing like it. Indeed, it is the most available democratic experience. We vote less than once a year. Only in church and at the polls are we actually given our supposed value, the soul-unit of one, with its noumenal arithmetic of equality: one equals one equals one.

My preaching corrupts the words and corrupts me. Belief

builds itself unconsciously and in consciousness is spent. Throughout my childhood I felt nothing in church but boredom and an oppressive futility. For reasons my father never explained, he was a dutiful churchman; my mother, who could use her senses, who had read Santayana and Wells, stayed home Sunday mornings, and I was all on her side, on the side of phenomena, in those years, though I went, with the other children, to Sunday school. It was not until we moved from the town and joined a country church that I, an adolescent of fifteen, my head a hotbed of girls and literature, felt a pleasant emotion in church. During Lent – that dull season, those forty gray days during which the earth prepares the resurrection that the church calendar seizes upon as conveniently emblematic – I ushered with my father at the Wednesday-night services. We would arrive in our old car – I think it was the '38 Chevrolet then – on those raw March nights and it pleasantly surprised me to find the building warm, the stoked furnace already humming its devotions in the basement. The nave was dimly lit, the congregation small, the sermon short, and the wind howled a nihilistic counterpoint beyond the black windows blotted with garbled apostles; the empty pews, making the minister seem remote and small and emblematic, intensified our sensation of huddling. There was a strong sepia flavor of early Christianity: a minority flock furtively gathered within a dying, sobbing empire. From the rear, the broad back and baked neck of the occasional dutiful son loomed bullishly above the black straw hats of the mischievous-looking old ladies, gnarled by farmwork, who sat in their rows like withered apples on the shelves of a sweet-smelling cellar. My father would cross and uncross and recross his legs and stare at his thoughts, which seemed distant. It was pleasant to sit beside him in the rear pew. He was not much of a man for sitting

182

still. When my parents and I went to the movies, he insisted on having the aisle seat, supposedly to give his legs room. After about twenty minutes he would leap up and spend the rest of the show walking around in the back of the theatre drinking water and talking to the manager while my mother and I, abandoned, consoled ourselves with the flickering giants of make-believe. He had nothing of the passive in him; a church always became, for him, something he helped run. It was pleasant, and even exciting, when the moment for action came, to walk by his side up the aisle, the thump of our feet the only sound in the church, and to take the wooden, felt-floored plates from a shy blur of white robes and to administer the submission of alms. Coins and envelopes sought to cover the felt. I condescended, stooping gallantly into each pew. The congregation seemed the Others, reaching, with quarters glittering in their fingers, toward mysteries in which I was snugly involved. Even to usher at a church mixes us with the angels, and is a dangerous thing.

The churches of Greenwich Village had this second-century quality. In Manhattan, Christianity is so feeble its future seems before it. One walks to church past clattering cafeterias and glowering news vendors in winter weather that is always a shade of Lent, on pavements spangled with last night's vomit. The expectantly hushed shelter of the church is like one of those spots worn bare by a softball game in a weed-filled vacant lot. The presence of the city beats like wind at the glowing windows. One hastens home afterward, head down, hurrying to assume the disguise – sweaters and khaki pants – of a non-churchgoer. I tried not to go, but it was not in me not to go. I never attended the same church two Sundays in succession, for fear I would become known and be expected. To be known by face and name and financial weight robs us of our unitary soul, enrolls us against those Others. Devil's work. We are the others. It is of the essence to be a stranger in church.

On the island the very color of my skin made me strange. This island had been abandoned to the descendants of its slaves. Their church was on a hill; it has since been demolished, I have learned from letters, by a hurricane. To reach it one climbed a steep path made treacherous by the loose rubble of coral rock, jagged gray clinkers that bore no visible relation to the pastel branches that could be plucked, still pliant, from the shallows by Maid's Beach. Dull-colored goats were tethered along the path; their forelegs were tangled in their ropes so tightly that whenever they nodded the bush anchoring them nodded in answer. For windows the church possessed tall arched apertures filled not with stained glass but with air and outward vision; one could see the goats stirring the low foliage and the brightly dressed little girls who had escaped the service playing on the packed dirt around the church. The service was fatiguingly long. There were exhaustive petitionary prayers (for the Queen, the Prime Minister, Parliament) and many eight-versed hymns sung with a penetrating, lingering joy and accompanied by a hand-pumped organ. The organ breathed in and out, loud and soft, and the congregation, largely female, followed its ebb and flow at a brief but noticeable distance; their lips moved behind the singing, so I seemed immersed in an imperfectly synchronized movie. Musical stress, the West Indian accent, and elision worked upon the words a triple distortion. "Lait eth's waadsa *cull* raio-ind . . ." Vainly seeking my place in the hymn – for without a visual key I was lost – I felt lifted within a warm, soughing milk, an aspiring chant as patient as the nodding of the goats.

Throughout the service, restless deacons slipped in and out of the windows. Bored myself – for we grow sated even with consolation – I discovered that without moving from my pew I too could escape through those tall portals built to admit the breeze. I rested my eyes on earth's wide circle round. From this height the horizon of the sea was lifted halfway up the sky. The Caribbean seemed a steeply tilted blue plane to which the few fishing boats in the bay below had been attached like magnetized toys. God made the world, Aquinas says, in play.

Matter has its radiance and its darkness; it lifts and it buries. Things compete; a life demands a life. On another English island, in Oxford – it is a strange fact about Americans, that we tend to receive our supernatural mail on foreign soil – I helped a cat die. The incident had the signature: decisive but illegible. For years I did not tell my wife about it, for fear it would frighten her. Some hours before, I had left her at the hospital in the early stages of labor. Wearing a sterilized gown and mask, I had visited her in a white-tiled room along whose walls gleaming gutters stood ready to drain torrents of blood. Her face, scrubbed and polished, was fervent like a child's, and she seemed, lying there swathed in white, ready for nothing so much as a graduation ceremony. She would break off talking, and listen as if to the distant voice of a schoolmistress, and her face would grow rapt, and when the contraction had passed she would sigh and say, "That was a good one," and chatter some more to me of how I would feed myself alone and to whom I would send telegrams.

Shooed from the room, stripped of my mask, I tried to wait, and was told, the comical useless husband of American cartoons, to run on home; it would be "a time." I went outside and took a bus home. It was the last day of March. I had been born in March, and had looked forward to welcoming my child to the month; but she was late. We lived on Iffley Road, and around midnight, for some reason – I think to mail a letter, but what letter could have been that important? – I was out walking a few blocks from our flat. The night was cold enough for gloves. The sensations of turning into a father (or, rather, the lack of sensations: the failure of sympathetic pain, the anesthetized dread, the postponement of pride) made the street seem insubstantial. There was not that swishing company of headlights that along an American road throws us into repeated relief. The brick homes, save for an occasional introverted glow in an upstairs window, were dark in their vehement English privacy behind the thatchy hedges and spiked walls. The streetlamps – wintry, reserved – drained color from everything. Myself a shadow, I noticed another in the center of the road. A puddle of black, as I watched, it curled on itself; its ends lifted from the macadam and seemed to stretch in a yawn. Then it became inert again. I was horrified; the shape was about the size of a baby. When it curled the second time, I went to it, my footsteps the only sound in the street.

It was a cat that had been struck by a car. Struck but not quite killed: a testament to the modest speed and sensible size of English automobiles. By the impersonal witness of the lamps burning in the trees I couldn't be sure what color its fur was – it seemed orange-yellow, tabbied with stripes of dark ginger. The cat was plump and wore a collar. Someone had loved it. Blackness from one ear obscured one side of its head and when I touched here it was like a cup. For the third time, the cat stretched, the tips of its hind feet quivering luxuriously in that way cats have. With a great spastic effort it flipped over onto its other side, but made no cry. The only sound between us was my crooning as I carried it to the side of the street and laid it behind the nearest hedge.

A sallow upstairs light in this home was glowing. I wondered if the cat was theirs. Was it their love invested in my hands? Were they watching as I pushed, crouching, with my burden through their hedge? I wondered if I would be taken for a trespasser; as an American, I was nervous of English taboos. In my own country it was a not uncommon insult to kill a cat and throw the body into an enemy's yard, and I was afraid that this might be taken that way. I thought of writing a note to explain everything, but I had no paper and pen. I explained to the cat, how I was taking her (I felt the cat was female) out of the street so no more cars would hit her, how I would put her here in the nice safe dirt behind the hedge, where she could rest and get well. I did not believe she would get well; I think she was dead already. Her weight had felt dead in my hands and when I laid her down she did not stretch or twitch again.

Back in my flat, I discovered that one glove was smeared with blood. Most of the palm and three of the fingers were dyed wine-brown. I hadn't realized there was so much blood. I took off my gloves and carefully wrote a note, explaining that I had found this cat in the middle of the street, still alive, and that I had put it behind this hedge to be safe. If, as I thought, the cat was dead, I hoped that the finders would bury it. After some deliberation, I signed my name and address. I walked back and tucked the note under the cat's body, which seemed at home behind the hedge; it suffered my intrusion a trifle stiffly. It suggested I was making too much fuss, and seemed to say to me, *Run on home*.

Back in my flat once more, I felt abruptly tired, though my heart was pounding. I went to bed and set the alarm for three and read a book. I remember the title, it was Chesterton's *The Everlasting Man*. I turned off the light and prayed for my wife and, though I did not believe myself capable of it, fell asleep. The alarm at three came crashing into some innocent walk of a dream and my frail head felt like a hollow cup. I dressed and went out to the public phone booth a block away and called the hospital. A chirping voice, after some rummaging in the records, told me that several hours ago, in the first hour of April (in the United States it was still March), a perfect female infant had been born. To me.

The next morning, after all the telegrams had been managed, I went back to the hedge, and the cat and my note were gone. Though I had left my address, I never received a letter.

When we returned from England, we bought a car. We had ordered it through my parents from folders they had sent us, and though its shade of blue was more naïve, more like a robin's egg, than we had expected, this '55 Ford proved an excellent buy. Whether being shuffled from side to side of West Eighty-fifth Street every morning or being rammed in second gear up a washed-out mountain road in Vermont, it never complained. In New York hot tar from a roof-patching job rained onto its innocent paint, and in Vermont its muffler was racked and rent on a shelf of rock, and in Massachusetts it wallowed, its hot clutch stinking, up from more than one grave of snow. Not only sand and candy wrappers accumulate in a car's interior, but heroisms and instants of communion. Americans make love in their cars, and listen to ball games, and plot their wooing of the dollar: small wonder the landscape is sacrificed to these dreaming vehicles of unitary personhood.

In the beginning, my wife and I would lovingly lave with soap and warm water the unflecked skin of the hood as if it were the thorax of a broad blue baby, and toward the end we let the gallant old heap rust where it would. Its eggshell finish grew grizzled with the stains of dropped maple seeds. Its doors balked at closing; its windows refused to roll down. But I somehow never believed we would ever trade it in, though the little girl born across the ocean in the ominous turning of April, now a vocal and status-conscious democrat of nearly six, applied more and more pressure. The deal was consummated while my soul had its face turned, and Detroit contracted to devour her offspring. But before the new car arrived, there was a month's grace, and in this grace I enjoyed a final fling with my car, my first, my only – for all the others will be substitutes. It happened this way:

Dancing at a party with a woman not my wife, I took the opportunity to turn her hand in mine and kiss her palm. For some time her thighs had been slithering against mine, and, between dances, she developed a nervous clumsy trick of lurching against me, on tiptoe, and rubbing her breasts against my forearm, which was braced across my chest as I held a cigarette. My first thought was that I might burn her; my second, that Nature in her gruff maternal way had arranged one of her opportunities – as my mother, when I was a child, would unpredictably determine to give me a birthday or Halloween party. Obediently I bowed my head and kissed my friend's moist palm. As it withdrew from the advance, her fingertips caressed my chin in the absent-minded manner of one fingering the muzzle of an importunate dog. The exchange transposed us into a higher key; I could hardly hear my own voice, and our dancing lost all connection with the music, and my hand explored her spine from a great aerial distance. Her back seemed mysteriously taut and hard; the body of a strange woman retains more of its mineral content, not yet being transmuted into memory. In a sheltered corner of the room we stopped dancing altogether and talked, and what I distinctly remember is how her hands, beneath the steady and opaque appraisal of her eyes, in agitation blindly sought mine and seized and softly gripped, with infantile instinct, my thumbs. Just my thumbs she held, and as we talked she moved them this way and that as if she were steering me. When I closed my eyes, the red darkness inside my lids was vibrant, and when I rejoined my wife, and held her to dance, she asked, "Why are you panting?"

After we got home, and surveyed our four children, and in bed read a few pages made unbearably brilliant by the afterglow of gin, and turned out the light, she surprised me by not turning her back. Alcohol, with its loosening effect, touches women more deeply than men in this respect; or perhaps, like a matched pair of tuning forks, I had set her vibrating. Irritated by whatever illicit stimulations, we took it out on each other.

To my regret, I survived the natural bliss of satiety – when each muscle is like a petal snugly curved within the corolla – and was projected onto the seething, azoic territory of insomnia. That feathery anxious embrace of my erect thumbs tormented me in twenty postures. My stomach turned in love of that woman; I feared I would be physically sick and lay on my back gingerly and tried to soothe myself with the caress of headlights as they evolved from bright slits on the wall into parabolically accelerating fans on the ceiling and then vanished: this phenomenon, with its intimations of a life beyond me, had comforted wakeful nights in my earliest childhood. It was small comfort now. In Sunday school long ago I had been struck by the passage in which Jesus says that to lust after a woman in thought is the same as committing adultery. I found myself helplessly containing the conviction that wishes, not deeds, are judged. To crave a sin was to commit it; to touch the brink was to be on the floor of the chasm. The universe that so easily permitted me to commit adultery became, by logical steps each one of which went more steeply down than the one above it, a universe that would easily permit me to die. The depths of cosmic space, the maddening distension of time, history's forgotten slaughters, the child smothered in the dumped icebox, the recent breakdown of the molecular life-spiral, the proven physiological roots of the mind, the presence in our midst of idiots, Eichmanns, animals, and bacteria – all this evidence piled on, and I seemed already eternally forgotten. The dark vibrating air of my bedroom felt like the dust of my grave; the dust went up and up and I prayed upward into it, prayed, prayed for a sign, any glimmer at all, any microscopic loophole or chink in the chain of evidence, and saw none. I remembered a movie that had frightened me as a child; in it Jimmy Cagney, moaning and struggling, is dragged on rubber legs down the long corridor to the electric chair. I was that condemned man. My brain in its calcium vault shouted about injustice, thundered accusations into the lustreless and tranquil homogeneity of the air. Each second that my protest went unanswered justified it more certainly: the God who permitted me this fear was unworthy of existence. Each instant that my terror was extended amplified God's non-existence, so, as the graph of certain equations fluctuates more and more widely as it moves along the lateral coördinate, or as the magnetic motive-power in atom-smashers accelerates itself, I was caught in a vortex whose unbearably shrill pitch moved me at last to drop my weight on my wife's body and beg, "Wake up, Elaine. I'm so frightened."

I told her of the centuries coming when our names would be forgotten, of the millennia when our nation would be a myth and our continent an ocean, of the aeons when our earth would have vanished and the stars themselves be diffused into a uniform and irreversible cold. As, an hour before, I had transferred my lust to her, so now I tried to pass my fear into her. It seemed to offend her sense of good taste that I was jealous of future aeons and frantic because I couldn't live through them; she asked me if I had never been so sick I gave up caring whether I lived or died. This contemptible answer – animal stoicism – acquired a curious reinforcement: eventually, just as I had during the birth of my first child, I fell asleep. In my dreams, I was back in high school, with people I hadn't seen for years.

The next day, a Saturday, was my birthday. It passed like any day except that underneath the camouflage of furniture and voices and habitual actions I felt death like a wide army advancing. The newspaper told of nothing but atrocities. My children, wounded and appalled in their competition, came to me to be comforted and I was dismayed to see myself, a gutted shell, appearing to them as the embodiment and pledge of a safe universe. Friends visited, and for the first time truly in my life I realized that each face is suppressing knowledge of an immense catastrophe; our faces are dams that wrinkle under the strain.

Around six the telephone rang. It was my mother calling from Pennsylvania. I assumed she had called because of my birthday, so I chattered humorously about the discomforts of growing old for a minute before she could tell me, her voice growing faint, the news. My father was in the hospital. He had been walking around with chest pains for two weeks and suffered shortness of breath at night. She had finally coaxed him into a doctor's office; the doctor had taken a cardiogram and driven him straight to the hospital. He was a seriously sick man.

Instantly I was relieved. All day death had been advancing under cover and now it had struck, declared its position. My father had engaged the enemy and it would be defeated.

I was restored to crisp health in the play-world of action. That night we had a few friends in for my birthday party, and the next day I took the two older children to Sunday school and went myself to church. The faintly violet lozenge-panes of the tall white windows glowed and dimmed fitfully. It was a spottily overcast day, spitting a little snow. While I was at church my wife had cooked a lamb dinner. As I drank the coffee it became clear that I must drive to Pennsylvania. My mother and I had agreed I would fly down and visit him in a few days; I would have to see about renting a car at the Philadelphia end. This was potentially awkward because, self-employed, I had no credit card. The awkwardness suddenly seemed easy to surmount. I would drive. The car would be traded in a few days; it had just been greased; I had a vision of escaping our foul New England spring by driving south. In half an hour my bag was packed. *Run on home.*

Along Route 128 I picked up a young sailor who rode with me all the way to New York and, for two hours through Connecticut, drove my car. I trusted him. He had the full body, the frank and fleshy blue-eyed face of the docile Titans – guileless, competent, mildly earnest – that we have fattened, an ocean removed from the slimming Latin passions and Nordic anxieties of Europe, on our unprecedented abundance of milk and honey, vitamins and protein. He was incongruously – and somehow reassuringly – tanned. He had got the tan in Key West, where he had spent twenty-four hours, hitching the rides to and from on Navy jets. He had spent the twenty-four hours sleeping on the beach and selecting souvenirs to send back to his parents and girlfriend. His parents lived in Salem, his girlfriend in Peabody. He wanted to marry her, but his parents had old-fashioned ideas, they thought he was too young. And a lot of these guys in the service say, Don't get married, don't ever get married. But she was a nice girl, not so pretty or anything, but really nice: he really wouldn't mind marrying her.

I asked him how old he was. He was twenty-two, and was being trained as an airplane mechanic. He wanted at the end of his hitch to come back to Salem and live. He figured an airplane mechanic could find some sort of job. I told him, with a paternal firmness that amazed my ears, to marry her; absolutely; his parents would get used to it. The thing about parents, I told him, was that secretly, no matter what you did, they liked you anyway. I told him I had married at the age of twenty-one and had never been sorry.

He asked me, "What do you do? Teach?"

This impressed me. My grandfather had been a teacher, and my father was a teacher, and from my childhood up it had been assumed by people that I in turn would become a teacher.

"No," I said. "I'm a writer."

He seemed less offended than puzzled. "What do you write?"

"Oh – whatever comes into my head."

"What's the point?"

"I don't know," I told him. "I wish I did. Maybe there are several points."

We talked less freely after that. At his request I left him off in wet twilight at a Texaco station near the entrance of the New Jersey Turnpike. He hoped to get a ride from there all the way to Washington. Other sailors were clustered out of the rain in the doorways of the station. They hailed him as if they had been waiting for him, and as he went to them he became, from the back, just one more sailor, anonymous, at sea. He did not turn and wave goodbye. I felt I had frightened him, which I regretted, because he had driven for me very well and I wanted him to marry his girl. In the dark

I drove down the pike alone. In the first years of my car, when we lived in Manhattan, it would creep up to seventy-five on this wide black stretch without our noticing; now the needle found its natural level at sixty. The windshield wipers beat, and the wonderland lights of the Newark refineries were swollen and broken like bubbles by the raindrops on the side windows. For a dozen seconds a cross of blinking stars was suspended in the upper part of the windshield: an airplane above me was coming in to land.

I did not eat until I was on Pennsylvania soil. The Howard Johnsons in Pennsylvania are cleaner, less crowded, more homelike in their furnishings. The decorative plants seem to be honestly growing, and the waitresses have just a day ago removed the Mennonite cap from their hair, which is still pulled into a smooth bun flattering to their pallid, sly faces. They served me with that swift grace that comes in a region where food is still one of the pleasures. The familiar and subtle irony of their smiles wakened in me that old sense, of Pennsylvania knowingness – of knowing, that is, that the truth is good. They were the innkeeper's daughters, God had given us crops, and my wagon was hitched outside.

When I returned to the car, the music on the radio had changed color. The ersatz hiccup and gravel of Atlantic Seaboard hillbilly had turned, inland, backwards into something younger. As I passed the Valley Forge intersection the radio played a Benny Goodman quintet that used to make my scalp freeze. The speedometer went up to seventy without effort.

I left the toll road for our local highway and, slowing to turn into our dirt road, I was nearly rammed from behind by a pair of headlights that had been pushing, Pennsylvania style, six feet behind me. I parked beside my father's car in front of the barn. My mother came unseen into the yard, and, two voices calling in the opaque drizzle, while the dogs yapped deliriously in their pen, we debated whether I should move my car farther off the road. "Out of harm's way," my grandfather would have said. Complaining, I obeyed her. My mother turned as I carried my suitcase down the path of sandstone steppingstones, and led me to the back door as if I would not know the way. So it was not until we were inside the house that I could kiss her in greeting. She poured us two glasses of wine. Wine had a ceremonial significance in our family; we drank it seldom. My mother seemed cheerful, even silly, and it took an hour for the willed good cheer to ebb away. She turned her head and looked delicately at the rug, and the side of her neck reddened as she told me, "Daddy says he's lost all his faith."

"Oh, my." Since I had also lost mine, I could find nothing else to say. I remembered, in the silence, a conversation I had had with my father during a vacation from college. With the habitual simplicity of his eagerness to know, he had asked me, "Have you ever had any doubts of the existence of a Divine Being?"

"Sure," I had answered.

"I never have," he said. "It's beyond my ability to imagine it. The divinity of Jesus, yes; but the existence of a Divine Being, never." He stated this not as an attempt to influence me, but as a moderately curious fact he had that moment discovered about himself.

"He never was much one for faith," my mother added, hurt by my failure to speak. "He was strictly a works man."

I slept badly; I missed my wife's body, that weight of memory, beside me. I was enough of a father to feel lost out of my nest of little rustling souls. I kept looking out of the windows. The three red lights of the chimneys of the plant that had been built some miles away, to mine low-grade iron ore, seemed to be advancing over our neighbor's ridged field toward our farm. My mother had mistaken me for a stoic like my father and had not put enough blankets on the bed. I found an old overcoat of his and arranged it over me; its collar scratched my chin. I tipped into sleep and awoke. The morning was sharply sunny; sheep hustled, heads toppling, through the gauzy blue sky. It was authentic spring in Pennsylvania. Some of the grass in the lawn had already grown shiny and lank. A yellow crocus had popped up beside the BEWARE OF THE DOG sign my father had had an art student at the high school make for him.

I insisted we drive to Alton in my car, and then was sorry, for it seemed to insult their own. Just a few months ago my father had traded in on yet one more second-hand car: now he owned a '53 Dodge. But while growing up I had been ambushed by so many mishaps in my father's cars that I insisted we take the car I could trust. Or perhaps it was that I did not wish to take my father's place behind the wheel of his car. My father's place was between me and Heaven; I was afraid of being placed adjacent to that far sky. First we visited his doctor. Our old doctor, a man who believed that people simply "wore out" and nothing could be done about it, had several years ago himself worn out and died. The new doctor's office, in the center of the city, was furnished with a certain raw sophistication. Rippling music leaked from the walls, which were hung with semi-professional oils. He himself was a wiry and firm-tongued young man not much older than myself but venerable with competence and witnessed pain. Such are the brisk shepherds who hop us over the final stile. He brought down from the top of a filing cabinet a plaster model of the human heart. "Your own heart," he told me, "is nice and thin like this; but your dad's heart is enlarged. We believe the obstruction is here, in one of these little vessels on the outside, luckily for your dad."

Outside, in the streets of Alton, my own heart felt enlarged. A white sun warmed the neat façades of painted brick; chimneys red like peony shoots thrust through budding treetops. Having grown accustomed to the cramped, improvised cities of New England, I was impressed, like a tourist, by Alton's straight broad streets and handsome institutions. While my mother went off to buy my daughter a birthday present – April was nearly upon us – I returned a book she had borrowed from the Alton Public Library. I had forgotten the deep aroma of that place, mixed of dust and cleaning fluid and binder's glue and pastry baking in the bakery next door. Revisiting the shelf of P. G. Wodehouse that I had once read straight through, I took down *Mulliner Nights* and looked in the back for the stamped date, in '47 or '48, that would be me. I never thought to look for the section of the shelves where my own few books would be placed. They were not me. They were my children, touchy and self-willed.

In driving to the hospital on Alton's outskirts, we passed the museum grounds, where every tree and flower-bed wore a name-tag and black swans drifted through flotillas of crumbled bread. As a child I had believed literally that bread cast upon the waters came back doubled. Within the museum there were mummies with lips snarling back from their teeth in astonishment; a tiny gilt chair for a baby pharaoh; an elephant tusk carved into hundreds of tiny Chinamen and pagodas and squat leafy trees; miniature Eskimo villages that you lit up with a switch and peeped into like an Easter egg; cases of arrowheads; rooms of stuffed birds; and, upstairs, dower chests decorated with hearts and unicorns and tulips by the pious "plain people," and iridescent glassware from the kilns of Baron von Stiegel, and slashing paintings of Pennsylvania woodland by the Shearer brothers, and bronze statuettes of wrestling Indians that stirred my first erotic dreams, and, in the round skylit room at the head of the marble stairs, a black-rimmed pool in whose center a naked green girl held to her pursed lips a shell whose transparent contents forever spilled from the other side, filling this whole vast upstairs – from whose Palladian windows the swans in their bready pond could be seen trailing fan-shaped wakes – with the trickle and splatter of falling water. The world then seemed to me an intricate wonder displayed for my delight with no price asked. Visible above the trees across the pond were rose glints of the hospital, an orderly multitude of tall brick rectangles set among levelled and well-tended grounds, an ideal city of the ill.

I had forgotten how grand the Alton hospital was. I had not seen its stately entrance, approached down a grassy mall, since, at the age of eight, I had left the hospital unburdened of my tonsils. Then, too, it had been spring, and the mall was bright with the first flush of green, and my mother was with me. I recalled it to her, and she said, "I felt so guilty. You were so sick."

"Really? I remember it as so pleasant." They had put a cup of pink rubber over my nose and there had been a thunderous flood of the smell of cotton candy and I opened my eyes and my mother was reading a magazine beside my bed.

"You were such a hopeful good boy," my mother said, and I did not look at her face for fear of seeing her crying.

I wondered aloud if a certain girl in my high-school class was still a nurse here.

"Oh, dear," my mother said. "Here I thought you came all this way to see your poor old father and all you care about is seeing –" And she used the girl's maiden name, though the girl had been married as long as I had.

Within the hospital, she surprised me by knowing the way. Usually, wherever we went, it was my father or I who knew the way. As I followed her through the linoleum maze, my mother's shoulders seemed already to have received the responsible shawl of widowhood. Like the halls of a palace, the hospital corridors were lined with petitioners, waiting for a verdict. Negro girls electrically dramatic in their starched white uniforms folded bales of cotton sheets; gray men pushed wrung mops. We went past an exit sign, down a stairway, into a realm where gaunt convalescents in bathrobes shuffled in and out of doorways. I saw my father diagonally through a doorway before we entered his room. He was sitting up in bed, supported sultanlike by a wealth of pillows and clad in red-striped pajamas.

I had never seen him in pajamas before; a great man for the shortest distance between two points, he slept in his underclothes. But, having been at last captured in pajamas, like a big-hearted lion he did not try to minimize his subdual, but lay fully exposed, without a sheet covering even his feet. Bare, they looked pale, thin-skinned, and oddly unused.

Except for a sullen lymphatic glow under his cheeks, his face was totally familiar. I had been afraid that his loss of faith would show, like the altered shape of his mouth after he had had all his teeth pulled. With grins we exchanged the shy handshake that my going off to college had forced upon us. I sat on the windowsill by his bed, my mother took the chair at the foot of the bed, and my father's roommate, a fortyish man flat on his back with a ruptured disc, sighed and blew smoke toward the ceiling and tried, I suppose, not to hear us. Our conversation, though things were radically changed, followed old patterns. Quite quickly the talk shifted from him to me. "I don't know how you do it, David," he said. "I couldn't do what you're doing if you paid me a million dollars a day." Embarrassed and flattered, as usual, I tried to shush him, and he disobediently turned to his roommate and called loudly, "I don't know where the kid gets his ideas. Not from his old man, I know that. I never gave the poor kid an idea in my life."

"Sure you did," I said softly, trying to take pressure off the man with the hurting back. "You taught me two things. One, always butter bread toward the edges because enough gets in the middle anyway; and, two, no matter what happens to you, it'll be a new experience."

To my dismay, this seemed to make him melancholy. "That's right, David," he said. "No matter what happens to you, it'll be a new experience. The only thing that worries me is that *she*" – he pointed at my mother – "will crack up the car. I don't want anything to happen to your mother."

"The car, you mean," my mother said, and to me she added, "It's a sin, the way he worships that car."

My father didn't deny it. "Jesus, I love that car," he said. "It's the first car I've ever owned that didn't go bad on me. Remember all those heaps we used to ride back and forth in?"

The old Chevy was always getting dirt in the fuel pump and refusing to start. Once, going down Firetown Hill, the left front wheel had broken off the axle; my father wrestled with the steering wheel while the tires screamed and the white posts of the guard fence floated toward my eyes. When the car slid sideways to a stop just short of the embankment, my father's face was stunned and the corners of his mouth dribbled saliva. I was surprised; it had not occurred to me to be frightened. The '36 Buick had drunk oil, a quart every fifty miles, and liked to have flat tires after midnight, when I would be sailing home with a scrubbed brain and the smell of lipstick in my nose. Once, when we had both gone into town and I had dropped him off and taken the car, I had absent-mindedly driven home alone. I came in the door and my mother said, "Why, where's your father?"

My stomach sank. "My Lord," I said, "I forgot I had him!"

As, smiling, I took in breath and prepared to dip with him into reminiscence of these adventures, my father, staring stonily into the air above his pale and motionless toes, said, "I love this place. There are a lot of wonderful gentlemen in here. The only thing that worries me is that Mother will crack up the car."

My mother was leaning forward pink-faced in the chair at the foot of the bed, trying to smile. He glanced at her and said to me, "It's a funny feeling. The night before we went to see the doctor, I woke up and couldn't get my breath and realized I wasn't ready to die. I had always thought I would be. It's a funny feeling."

"Luckily for your dad," "all his faith," "wonderful gentlemen": these phrases were borne in on me, and my tongue seemed pressed flat on the floor of its grave. The pajama stripes under my eyes stirred and streamed, real blood. I wanted to speak, to say how I still needed him and to beg him not to leave me, but there were no words, no form of words available in our tradition. A pillar of smoke poured upward from the sighing man in the other bed.

Into this pit hesitantly walked a plain, painfully clean girl with a pad and pencil. She had yellow hair, thick lips, and, behind pink-rimmed glasses, large eyes that looked as if they had been corrected from being crossed. They flicked across our faces and focused straight ahead in that tunnel-vision gaze of those who know perfectly well they are figures of fun; the Jehovah's Witnesses who come to the door wear that guarded expression. She approached the bed where my father lay barefoot and, suppressing a stammer, explained that she was from Lutheran Home Missions and that they kept accounts of all hospitalized Lutherans and notified the appropriate pastors to make visitations. Perhaps she had measured my father for a rebuff. Perhaps her eyes, more practiced in this respect than mine, spotted the external signs of loss of faith that I couldn't see. At any rate my father was a Lutheran by adoption; he had been born and raised a Presbyterian and still looked like one.

"That's *aw*fully nice of you," he told the girl. "I don't see how you people do it on the little money we give you."

Puzzled, she dimpled and moved ahead with her routine. "Your church is – ?"

He told her, pronouncing every syllable meticulously and consulting my mother and me as to whether the word "Evangelical" figured in the official title.

"That would make your pastor Reverend –"

"Yeah. He'll be in, don't worry about it. Wild horses couldn't keep him away. Nothing he likes better than to get out of the sticks and drive into Alton. I didn't mean to confuse you a minute ago; what I meant was, just last week in church council we were talking about you people. We couldn't figure out how you do anything on the little money we give you. After we've got done feeding the furnace and converting the benighted Hindu there isn't anything left over for you people that are trying to help the poor devils in our own back yard."

The grinning girl was lost in this onslaught of praise and clung to the shreds of her routine. "In the meantime," she recited, "here is a pamphlet you might like to read."

My father took it from her with a swooping gesture so expansive I got down from the windowsill to restrain him physically, if necessary. That he must lie still was my one lever, my one certainty about his situation. "That's awfully nice of you," he told the girl. "I don't know where the hell you get the money to print these things."

"We hope your stay in the hospital is pleasant and would like to wish you a speedy recovery to full health."

"Thank you; I know you're sincere when you say it. As I was telling my son David here, if I can do what the doctors tell me I'll be all right. First time in my life I've ever tried to do what anybody ever told me to do. The kid was just telling me, 'No matter what happens to you, Pop, it'll be a new experience.'"

"Now, if you will excuse me, I have other calls to pay."

"Of course. You go right ahead, sick Lutherans are a dime a dozen. You're a wonderful woman to be doing what you're doing."

And she left the room transformed into just that. As a star shines in our Heaven though it has vanished from the universe, so my father continued to shed faith upon others. For the remainder of my visit with him his simple presence so reassured me, filled me with such a buoyant humor, that my mother surprised me, when we had left the hospital, by remarking that we had tired him.

"I hadn't noticed," I said.

"And it worries me," she went on, "the way he talks about the movies all the time. You know he never liked them." When I had offered to stay another night so I could visit him again, he had said, "No, instead of that why don't you take your mother tomorrow to the movies?" Rather than do that, I said, I would drive home. It took him a moment, it seemed, to realize that by my home I meant a far place, where I had a wife and children, dental appointments and work obligations. Though at the time I was impatient to have his consent to leave, it has since occurred to me that during that instant when his face was blank he was swallowing the realization that he could die and my life would go on. Having swallowed, he told me how good I had been to come all this way to see him. He told me I was a good son and a good father; he clasped my hand. I felt I would ascend straight north from his touch.

I drove my mother back to her farm and got my bag and said goodbye on the lawn. The little sandstone house was pink in the declining sunlight; the lawn was a tinkling clutter of shy rivulets. Standing beside the BEWARE OF THE DOG sign with its companion of a crocus, she smiled and said, "This is like when you were born. Your father drove through a snowstorm all the way from Wheeling in our old Model A." He had been working with the telephone company then; the story of his all-night ride was the oldest narrative in which I was a character.

Darkness did not fall until New Jersey. The hour of countryside I saw from the Pennsylvania Turnpike looked enchanted – the branches of the trees underpainted with budding russet, the meadows nubbled like new carpets, the bronze sun slanting on Valley Forge and Levittown alike. I do not know what it is that is so welcome to me in the Pennsylvania landscape, but it is the same quality – perhaps of reposing in the certainty that the truth is good – that exists in Pennsylvania faces. It seemed to me for this sunset hour that the world is our bride, given to us to love, and the terror and joy of the marriage is that we bring to it a nature not our bride's.

There was no sailor to help me drive the nine hours back. New Jersey began in twilight and ended in darkness, and Manhattan made its gossamer splash at show-time hour, eight o'clock. The rest of the trip was more and more steeply uphill. The Merritt Parkway seemed meaninglessly coquettish, the light-controlled stretch below Hartford maddeningly obstinate, and the hour above that frighteningly empty. Distance grew thicker and thicker; the intricate and effortful mechanics of the engine, the stellar infinity of explosive sparks needed to drive it, passed into my body, and wearied me. Repeatedly I stopped for coffee and the hallucinatory comfort of human faces, and after every stop my waiting car, companion and haven and willing steed, responded to my pressure. It began to seem a miracle that the car could gather speed from my numb foot; the very music on the radio seemed a drag on our effort, and I turned it off, obliterating earthly time. We climbed through a space fretted by scattered brilliance and bathed in a monotonous wind. I had been driving forever; houses, furniture, churches, women were all things I had innocently dreamed. And through those aeons my car, beginning as a mechanical assembly of molecules, evolved into something soft and organic and consciously brave. I lost first heart, then head, and finally any sense of my body. In the last hour of the trip I ceased to care or feel or in any real sense see, but the car, though its soul the driver had died, maintained steady forward motion, and completed the journey safely. Above my back yard the stars were frozen in place, and the shapes of my neighbors' houses wore the wonder that children induce by whirling.

Any day now we will trade it in; we are just waiting for the phone to ring. I know how it will be. My father traded in many cars. It happens so cleanly, before you expect it. He would drive off in the old car up the dirt road exactly as usual, and when he returned the car would be new to us, and the old was gone, gone, utterly dissolved back into the mineral world from which it was conjured, dismissed without a blessing, a kiss, a testament, or any ceremony of farewell. We in America need ceremonies, is I suppose, sailor, the point of what I have written.

# IN FOOTBALL
# SEASON

DO YOU REMEMBER a fragrance girls acquire in autumn? As you walk beside them after school, they tighten their arms about their books and bend their heads forward to give a more flattering attention to your words, and in the little intimate area thus formed, carved into the clear air by an implicit crescent, there is a complex fragrance woven of tobacco, powder, lipstick, rinsed hair, and that perhaps imaginary and certainly elusive scent that wool, whether in the lapels of a jacket or the nap of a sweater, seems to yield when the cloudless fall sky like the blue bell of a vacuum lifts toward itself the glad exhalations of all things. This fragrance, so faint and flirtatious on those afternoon walks through the dry leaves, would be banked a thousandfold on the dark slope of the stadium when, Friday nights, we played football in the city.

"We" – we the school. A suburban school, we rented for some of our home games the stadium of a college in the city of Alton three miles away. My father, a teacher, was active in the Olinger High athletic department, and I, waiting for him beside half-open doors of varnished wood and frosted glass, overheard arguments and felt the wind of the worries that accompanied this bold and at that time unprecedented decision. Later, many of the other county high schools followed our lead; for the decision was vindicated. The stadium each Friday night when we played was filled. Not only students and parents came but spectators unconnected with either school, and the money left over when the stadium rent was paid supported our entire athletic program. I remember the smell of the grass crushed by footsteps behind the end zones. The smell was more vivid than that of a meadow, and in the blue electric glare the green vibrated as if excited, like a child, by being allowed up late. I remember my father taking tickets at the far corner of the wall, wedged into a tiny wooden booth that made him seem somewhat magical, like a troll. And of course I remember the way we, the students, with all of our jealousies and antipathies and deformities, would be – beauty and boob, sexpot and grind – crushed together like flowers pressed to yield to the black sky a concentrated homage, an incense, of cosmetics, cigarette smoke, warmed wool, hot dogs, and the tang, both animal and metallic, of clean hair. In a hoarse olfactory shout, these odors ascended. A dense haze gathered along the ceiling of brightness at the upper limit of the arc lights, whose glare blotted out the stars and made the sky seem romantically void and intimately near, like the death that now and then stooped and plucked one of us out of a crumpled automobile. If we went to the back row and stood on the bench there, we could look over the stone lip of the stadium down into the houses of the city, and feel the cold November air like the black presence of the ocean beyond the rail of a ship; and when we left after the game and from the hushed residential streets of this part of the city saw behind us a great vessel steaming with light, the arches of the colonnades blazing like portholes, the stadium seemed a great ship sinking and we the survivors of a celebrated disaster.

To keep our courage up, we sang songs, usually the same song, the one whose primal verse runs,

> Oh, you can't get to Heaven
> (*Oh, you can't get to Heaven*)

In a rocking chair
   (*In a rocking chair*),
'Cause the Lord don't want
   (*'Cause the Lord don't want*)
No lazy people there!
   (*No lazy people there!*)

And then repeated, double time. It was a song for eternity; when we ran out of verses, I would make them up:

Oh, you can't get to Heaven
   (*Oh, you can't get to Heaven*)
In Smokey's Ford
   (*In Smokey's Ford*)
'Cause the cylinders
   (*'Cause the cylinders*)
Have to be rebored.
   (*Have to be rebored.*)

Down through the nice residential section, on through the not-so-nice and the shopping district, past dark churches where stained-glass windows, facing inward, warned us with left-handed blessings, down Warren Avenue to the Running Horse Bridge, and across the bridge we walked, then two miles up the Alton Pike to Olinger, following the trolley tracks. My invention would become reckless:

Oh, you can't get to Heaven
   (*Oh, you can't get to Heaven*)
In a motel bed
   (*In a motel bed*)
'Cause the sky is blue
   (*'Cause the sky is blue*)
And the sheets are red.
   (*And the sheets are red.*)

Few of us had a license to drive, and fewer still had visited a motel. We were at that innocent age, on the borderline of sixteen, when damnation seems a delicious promise. There was Mary Louise Hornberger, who was tall and held herself with such upright and defiant poise that she was Mother in both our class plays, and Alma Bidding, with her hook nose and her smug smile caricatured in cerise lipstick, and Joanne Hardt, whose father was a typesetter, and Marilyn Wenrich, who had a gray front tooth and in study hall liked to have the small of her back scratched, and Nanette Seifert, with her button nose and black wet eyes and peach-down cheeks framed in the white fur frilling the blue hood of her parka. And there were boys – Henny Gring, Leo Horst, Hawley Peters, Jack Lillijedahl, myself. Sometimes these, sometimes less or more. Once there was Billy Trupp on crutches. Billy played football and, though only a sophomore, had made the varsity that year, until he broke his ankle. He was dull and dogged and liked Alma, and she with her painted smile led him on lovingly. We offered for his sake to take the trolley, but he had already refused a car ride back to Olinger and obstinately walked with us, loping his heavy body along on the crutches, his lifted foot a boulder of plaster. His heroism infected us all; we taunted the cold stars with song, one mile, two miles, three miles. How slowly we went! With what a luxurious sense of waste did we abuse this stretch of time! For as children we had lived in a tight world of ticking clocks and punctual bells, where every minute was an admonition to thrift and where tardiness, to a child running late down a street with his panicked stomach burning, seemed the most mysterious and awful of sins. Now, turning the corner into adulthood, we found time to be instead a black immensity endlessly supplied, like the wind.

We would arrive in Olinger after the drugstores, which

had kept open for the first waves of people returning from the game, were shut. Except for the streetlights, the town was dark; it was betranced, like a town in a fable. We scattered, each escorting a girl to her door; and there, perhaps, for a moment, you bowed your face into that silent crescent of fragrance, and tasted it, and let it bite into you indelibly. The other day, in a town far from Olinger, I passed on the sidewalk two girls utterly unknown to me and half my age, and sensed, very faintly, that flavor from far off carried in their bent arms like a bouquet. And, continuing to walk, I felt myself sink into a chasm deeper than the one inverted above us on those Friday nights during football season.

After seeing the girl home, I would stride through the hushed streets, where the rustling leaves seemed torn scraps scattered in the wake of the game, and go to Mr. Lloyd Stephens' house. There, looking in the little square window of his front storm door, I could see down a dark hall into the lit kitchen where Mr. Stephens and my father and Mr. Jesse Honneger were counting money around a worn porcelain table. Stephens, a local contractor, was the school-board treasurer, and Honneger, who taught social science, was chairman of the high-school athletic department. They were still counting; the silver stacks slipped and glinted among their fingers, and the gold of beer stood in cylinders beside their hairy wrists. Their sleeves were rolled up. Smoke, like a fourth presence, wings spread, hung over their heads. They were still counting, so it was all right. I was not late. We lived ten miles away, and I could not go home until my father was ready. Some nights it took until midnight. I would knock and pull open the storm door and push open the real door and it would be warm in the contractor's hall. I would accept a glass of ginger ale and sit in the kitchen with the men until they were done. It was late, very late, but I was not blamed;

it was permitted. Silently counting and expertly tamping the coins into little cylindrical wrappers of colored paper, the men ordered and consecrated this realm of night into which my days had never extended before. The hour or more behind me, which I had spent so wastefully, in walking when a trolley would have been swifter, and so wickedly, in blasphemy and lust, was past and forgiven me; it had been necessary; it was permitted.

Now I peek into windows and open doors and do not find that air of permission. It has fled the world. Girls walk by me carrying their invisible bouquets from fields still steeped in grace, and I look up in the manner of one who follows with his eyes the passage of a hearse, and remembers what pierces him.

# ACKNOWLEDGMENTS

These eleven stories originally appeared in *The New Yorker*. "The Alligators," "Friends from Philadelphia," and "The Happiest I've Been" were first collected in John Updike's book *The Same Door* (1959). "You'll Never Know, Dear, How Much I Love You," "Pigeon Feathers," "A Sense of Shelter," "Flight," "The Persistence of Desire," "The Blessed Man of Boston, My Grandmother's Thimble, and Fanning Island," and "Packed Dirt, Churchgoing, a Dying Cat, a Traded Car" were first collected in *Pigeon Feathers and Other Stories* (1962). "In Football Season" was first collected in the Vintage edition of *Olinger Stories* (1964) and was reprinted in *The Music School* (1966). The texts used here have been taken from *The Early Stories: 1953–1975* (2003).

The "barefaced reminiscence" quoted from on page 13 is John Updike's "The Dogwood Tree: A Boyhood" (1962), collected in his volume *Assorted Prose* (1965). The passage of italicized French on pages 174–5 is Blaise Pascal's Pensée No. 199 (1660).

Everyman's Library and the John H. Updike Literary Trust would like to thank Christopher Carduff for his help in preparing this edition of *Olinger Stories*.